DRIFT AWAY

DRIFT AWAY

A LIBBY KINCAID MYSTERY

KERRY TUCKER

HarperCollins*Publishers*

HarperCollins books may be purchased for educational, business, or sales promotional use. For information, please call or write: Special Markets Department, HarperCollins Publishers, Inc., 10 East 53rd Street, New York, NY 10022.

FIRST EDITION

Designed by R. Caitlin Daniels

Library of Congress Cataloging-in-Publication Data

Tucker, Kerry
   Drift away : a Libby Kincaid mystery / Kerry Tucker.
     p. cm.
   ISBN 0-06-017999-6
   1. Kincaid, Libby (Fictitious character)—Fiction. 2. Women photographers—Massachusetts—Boston—Fiction. 3. Boston (Mass.)—Fiction. I. Title.
PS3570.U34D75 1994
813'.54—dc20   94-17113

94 95 96 97 98 ❖/HC 10 9 8 7 6 5 4 3 2 1

To the memory of Ali Shah.

1

IT WAS THE FIRST DAY OF SPRING AND I WAS PINNED INTO A PAY-TV chair—the only space available in the Trailways station in Providence, Rhode Island. For the uninitiated—say, those whose cars don't lose their exhaust systems on I-95—a pay-TV chair is like the chair they put you in at the lab when they take blood out of you except the restraining arm has a television, usually jammed on one station, bolted to it. This particular model also featured choice words relating to the female anatomy carved with car keys or maybe a switchblade onto the control panel.

The next bus to Manhattan, where I live, wouldn't leave for an hour. I shoved my money into the slot and caught the last few minutes of a Spanish-language version of "The Dating Game." The woman in the unit next to mine poured some Pepsi into a bottle for her baby, twisted the nipple on, and shifted so she could see my screen; her pay-TV didn't work, or maybe she didn't think it was worth three bucks to watch a bunch of studs in tight pants talk about themselves.

"Okay if I watch?" she asked.

"Yeah, it's okay."

A couple of kids with fancy sneakers and shaved heads saw the screen light up and pulled up behind my chair. Almost unconsciously I palpated my jacket for my camera—I'd lost my beloved Leica three months before to a couple of guys like that.

One of them reached over my shoulder and slammed the channel dial with the butt of his fist. I lurched from the chair.

"Hey you little punks—what do you think—"

It was a newscast. A woman reporter peered out of a dark space toward the camera.

". . . for Andrea Hale, LeClair's attorney," she said. My stomach tightened. The punks were laughing and talking loud.

Andrea Hale? My Andrea Hale?

"Shut up," I said. "I've got to—"

The woman's voice was rawer than a TV reporter's voice is supposed to be.

"Authorities say Hale was last seen entering a conference room at Wessex County Courthouse with her client Mark LeClair—the conference room from which she may have helped him escape. LeClair was standing trial on charges of rape and murder of Edith Davis, a seventy-eight-year-old Grafton woman whose body was found last September in the basement of her home. Sources say that during a break in the trial Hale told a court officer that she was ill; she and LeClair apparently left the courthouse while the guard sought medical help for her. Authorities also say that a love letter in what appears to be Hale's handwriting was found among Hale's papers in the courtroom."

A massive creaking sound erupted from the TV. The cam-

2

era shook through darkness, trying to find the source of the noise. It came from an elevator—an enormous cage of black iron that descended as slowly as the night, swaying with the weight it carried, finally hitting the pavement with a shriek and a bang.

Police lights pulsed toward the cage, teasing out the back-side outline of a car, brown, maybe dark red.

The camera returned to the reporter.

"It was only half an hour ago," she continued, "that Andrea Hale's belongings were found in the backseat of . . . "

The woman gasped. The camera reeled from her face to the car. Police bent over the open trunk.

"No," the reporter said. "I don't want to . . . "

Now a body was on a stretcher, sideways, it seemed, and small, legs drawn to the chin perhaps, locked in a fetal pose. It was covered by a sheet, but one hand, the wrist encircled by a gold bracelet, dangled free.

I started shaking.

"I can't believe it," I heard myself say aloud to the woman with the baby. "I just can't . . . "

The kids in the sneakers backed away.

"I mean I went to school with her. We had an apartment together. I haven't seen her in a long time, but she was my friend. She wouldn't . . . "

The reporter, her voice hushed, finished her valediction.

"—for Newscenter Three, coming to you live from the Automatic Garage on Boston's Long Wharf."

The baby started to cry.

The woman pulled a diaper from a plastic bag and shook it open.

"Yeah?" she said. "Well it looks like she got herself in some real big shit."

2

I CALLED JACK HALE, ANDREA'S HUSBAND, THE NEXT DAY AND THE next and the next. At first the line was always busy, then no one answered, then I stopped trying. After all, I hadn't bothered getting in touch with either Andrea or Jack for the past eleven years; who was I to impose on a widower's grief? I wrote him a note to say I was sorry about the news and left it at that.

I bought both Boston papers to follow the story. The *Herald* was almost gleeful: "DID SHE OR DIDN'T SHE? HALE EX-HIPPIE, WALKED ON WILD SIDE." The *Globe* was more somber: "UNANSWERED QUESTIONS IN CASE OF DEAD ATTORNEY." There were lots of photographs: one was of Andrea giving the student address at her law school graduation years ago, dangling peace symbol earrings mingled with her beautiful, unruly, shoulder-length red-gold hair; another was of Andrea with her little brother, Patrick—he must have been thirteen or so at the time—the day they climbed the last mountain in New Hampshire that qualified them for the Appalachian Mountain Club's 4000 Footer Club.

The picture that the papers printed biggest and the news magazines picked up most was of Andrea at thirty-five or thirty-six, her hair now short, smooth, and tucked behind one ear to reveal a heavy curve of pearl and gold earring, smiling radiantly on the steps of the Federal District Courthouse in Boston, answering questions from reporters about her heavyweight victory over the manufacturers of a defective infant heart monitor.

I cried when I saw the short, ugly piece *Americans*, the magazine I work for, ran, headlined "WOMEN WHO LOVE MEN WHO KILL." ("You're taking your work too personally," my boss, Octavia, said. "Toughen up.") But there was little new information beyond what the reporter had said the day Andrea's body was found—the note, the escape, the body. Then after two or three weeks the pictures and articles stopped; Andrea's death was eclipsed in the Boston papers by the news that a stockbroker had opened fire in his downtown office, killing seven people, including the mayor's nephew. I canceled my subscriptions and laid the clippings to rest in the box where I keep memorabilia—my Girl Scout sash and the badges I never sewed on it; the newspaper picture of my dad, Max, collecting his first BigBucks check from the Ohio Lottery; and some snapshots of Lucas, my dog, from before he lost his leg.

Then spring went by, summer started, and my life careened, like a runaway car, into one of those periods—foreshadowed, it seems to me now, by Andrea's death—where everything that had been predictable and safe wasn't predictable and safe anymore: I got held up at knifepoint on a Saturday afternoon in Washington Square Park; Claire, my roommate, got pregnant and started talking about selling the loft we live in; and Dan Sikora, my comfortable, easygoing, conveniently long-distance boyfriend, started talking about getting married. To me. He said he wanted to have kids while he could still bend over to pick them up.

When I freaked—"Marriage? Are you kidding? I'm not ready; I need time—" he told me he didn't want to see me anymore.

I felt stripped, abandoned—like those burned-out cars and appliances you see dumped on the Cross-Bronx Expressway.

Claire, as usual, but with a swelling stomach, not as usual, retreated to her mother's in Maine for the summer. I stayed on Canal Street, went into my usual summer housekeeping slump, and concentrated on getting my work done, figuring out where to live next, and keeping my head screwed on. If Max ever paid back the money I'd loaned him I'd be able to make a down payment on a place of my own—nothing fancy, but space big enough for a darkroom and a bed, and maybe with the view of the Empire State Building I've always wanted.

As it was, I didn't even know where Max was. The last I'd talked with him was the September before, when he'd called from what he said was a truckstop in Breezewood, Pennsylvania. He said he was on his way to Florida and promised to send me his new address when he got there. Since then he'd sent me postcards from Weeki Wachee Springs (of bathing beauties smoking underwater); Disney World; and the *Love Boat*, which he said he was about to take a cruise on—but no address.

Then the day came when Claire phoned to tell me that a real estate broker would be showing up that afternoon to take a look at "the property." That's what Claire started calling the loft when she first got the notion of selling it. She used to call it "home," or "our place," or "Rancho Canal." Now it was "the property."

6

"Don't worry," she'd said. "It's just a preliminary. A pre-preliminary. Honest. Only to get an idea of what it would take to sell the property. Whether I'd need to paint it."

I couldn't think of anything nice to say, so I didn't say anything at all.

"I know it's hard for you to think about, Libby. But don't worry. Things aren't moving fast at all. I just need to know what to do to make it market ready."

Pre-preliminary. Market ready. Claire never used to talk this way. Maybe it was pregnancy hormones.

"So if you could just spiff it up a little. You don't have to wash the floors or anything. Just—"

Spiff it up. I picked up a Roach Motel and looked inside. No vacancies.

"She's coming at three. With a man from the bank."

My glance swung from the five-foot pile of laundry stacked by the washer-dryer to the kitchen ceiling lamp filled with the shadowy corpses of dead bugs to the tumbleweed-size dust-balls that coasted around the legs of the sofa. It was two-fifteen, and I was beginning to sweat. I mean, did I even *have* any Fantastik spray cleaner?

"Sure, Claire. Gotta go."

I could feel an adrenaline surge coming on.

I'm thirty-seven years old. (Dragging the Electrolux out of the closet).

My city has turned on me. (Extricating the electrical cord from a thicket of metal coat hangers.)

My friends and family have abandoned me. (Crawling behind the couch to find the outlet.)

I am a successful photographer— (Realizing that the vacuum isn't working because the bag is full, and that there are no new bags.)

—and I own nothing. (Stuffing the vacuum back in the closet and searching for a broom.)

7

They sell this joint tomorrow and I'm on the street. (Picking the dustballs out of the broom, then picking them off my sweating hands.)

My fax machine started to hum; a sheet of paper eased out of the slot and curled itself into the receiving tray.

Probably a command from Octavia.

I snatched the paper out of the tray.

The fax was on Harvard University letterhead: reserved typography, no zip code, some kind of heraldic device with animals on it.

The message beneath was handwritten in a big, clumsy scrawl.

> Hey Libby—
> Tony Stefko canceled. Can you be in
> Cambridge by Sept. 1?

My head felt light. Like it had just turned into a helium balloon.

I turned the paper over, wrote my response in letters three inches high, and sent it zinging through the phone lines— over the Long Island Sound, across the Connecticut tobacco fields, into the land of the bean and the cod.

YES, the wires sang.

YES. YES. YES.

3

THAT'S HOW I FOUND MYSELF, COME AUTUMN, IN CAMBRIDGE, MAS-
sachusetts, subletting an apartment between Porter Square
and Harvard Square and guest lecturing undergrads on the
history of photojournalism, or, as we billed the course:
"Objective and Subjective Reality: American Documentary
Photography, 1890 to 1950." I liked teaching the seminar; it
brought out the performer in me that I thought had been
embalmed by two decades of solitary darkroom work.

Octavia was skeptical at first—"Harvard, Olivia? Really?
Are you sure you're ready for that?"—but was enchanted
once she realized that she had a backlog of completed assignments from me and that she could take me off the magazine's
health benefits for a few months. "And Olivia," she'd said,
scrutinizing the chronic circles under my eyes, "the rest will
do you worlds of good. You'll come back ready to work
harder than ever!"

The good thing about the apartment was that I could have my dog, Lucas, with me and that it was only a half-hour walk from the building where I taught my seminar. The bad thing about it was that the guy I was renting from, a South African psychiatrist who specializes in people who have had previous lives, moved in with me two months after I landed there.

I'd gotten the place through a classified in the *New York Review of Books*. The ad said "perfect for visiting prof. Skylights. Water bed. Garden." The psychiatrist, who sounded nice enough on the phone, was moving in with his girlfriend but needed to make payments on the lease through June.

And it was perfect for visiting prof. At first, anyway. Lucas and I came up from Manhattan a week before I was supposed to start teaching and settled in. I scraped the scum off the skylights. Picked the cigarette butts out of the garden. Got my lectures in order. Got used to the idea of the water bed. Bought a pot of mums, plunked it by the front door, and congratulated myself on my new-found domesticity.

The neighborhood turned beautiful in the fall. It had been so many years since I'd lived anywhere near a tree that I found myself inordinately moved by the sight of the maple leaves that filled the front living room window turning peach, then hot orange, then dead and gone. For the first time since I was a little girl I had a slow-pulsed daily routine that approached the conventional: breakfast at home with the newspaper; walk to school with Lucas; walk back from school with Lucas and over to Fresh Pond Reservoir; make a sandwich; see a movie, maybe; prepare for class. September to October to November. Mathew Brady to Walker Evans to Weegee.

Then my landlord started coming around to visit.

At first it seemed okay. He needed to pick up his mail. He needed a certain book. He needed his cordless electric screwdriver. He was in the neighborhood and needed to pee.

Then he started hanging around talking. Eating food from out of the refrigerator. *My* food from out of the refrigerator. An entire ricotta pie from the North End.

Making phone calls. *Long* phone calls. Sitting down to read the newspaper. *My* newspaper.

Lucas hated him. He'd narrow his eyes and pace around the kitchen the whole time the guy was there.

So would I.

Then came the evening when I was sitting in a T-shirt and underpants on my bed, taking notes from a biography of Marion Post Wolcott for one of my lectures, and Altman showed up at my door. Not the front door. The bedroom door.

The conversation went something like this:

"Miss Kincaid—"

"Jesus! Altman! What are you doing here? Lucas—it's okay. Down boy!"

"My friend and I are having some difficulties. I'm going to have to spend the night here. Maybe a few nights."

"What are you talking about? You can't do that! This is *my* apartment. Ask a lawyer. Ask call-in radio. Ask *me*! What are you—nuts?"

His whipped off his glasses and looked at me with intense disappointment.

"I'll let that remark pass," he said. "I had thought you were a different kind of person."

He sat on the edge of the bed.

I stood up and pulled on my jeans.

He made a sweeping gesture around the room with one hand and smiled at me.

"I hope you're not thinking of this as a landlord and tenant relationship," he said. "I have no more claim to this"—he searched for the word—"life-space"—life-space?—"than you do. We're all tenants, after a fashion, every one of us. We all live in borrowed space, even if we've paid vast amounts of money for it, and we all live in borrowed time. I thought surely you, an artist, would understand this."

"You mean you think it should be okay with me if you move back while I'm still here? After you advertised this place and you took a deposit and a month's rent from me? When we're both grown-ups?"

He stared at me. His hands were twitching.

I started to sweat. I mean, I was only eight when I read the *Life* magazine article about Richard Speck, but I remember it very clearly.

"I won't sleep in the bed with you," he said. "I'll sleep on the couch."

I recalled that the only student nurse who survived rolled under the bed and played dead.

I looked at the water bed. No rolling space there; the wooden platform that held the mattress went straight down to the floor.

"I'm going for a walk," I said.

I clipped Lucas's leash to his collar, grabbed my wallet and camera, and headed for the front door.

When I was on the porch side of the threshold I put my head back in the apartment.

"One more thing, Altman," I said. "If you're not gone when I get back I'm calling the cops."

4

I<small>T WAS TEN WHEN</small> I <small>GOT TO</small> H<small>ARVARD</small> S<small>QUARE.</small> T<small>HE WEATHER WAS</small> oddly warm for November, and the place was infested with students, most of the girls wearing huge black combat boots and gossamer dresses, the guys in huge black combat boots, black pants, and retro-shirts with the top button buttoned. It was sort of like the clothes we wore in Rochester in the seventies—the peasant skirts combined with the Eisenhower jackets—but somehow this look was fiercer. Shriller, maybe. No flowers in anybody's hair. No funny floppy hats. No beads. More an atmosphere of hostility than freedom. Or was I remembering the good old days wrong?

I banged a can of Coke out of a machine next to the newsstand and sat down on a concrete wall, furious with myself for not having called the cops as soon as Altman showed up in my bedroom. A couple of kids in fake tie-dye stood under a bookstore awning playing guitars and singing Simon and

Garfunkel songs. They were terrible. In New York someone would have stabbed them. Here the crowd was swaying and smiling on the sidewalk.

Lucas started to moan along with the music and I dragged him down the street to something better: a juggler juggling an apple, a lighted torch, and a turned-on chain saw.

We sat on another part of the wall.

"Get a load of this, Lucas," I muttered to him. "The guy needed a place to stay, so I left the apartment. Brilliant, huh? What are we going to do? Sleep in the car? Under a bridge?"

The juggler, now on a unicycle, was trying to convince a little boy to climb up on his shoulders. The child wouldn't have any part of it.

Smart kid, I thought.

Somebody tapped me on the arm and I turned around. It was a nice-looking lady with a sleeping baby in a backpack. In one hand she was carrying a huge paper bag that said CRATE AND BARREL on it and in the other hand was a paper cone of flowers. She looked worried.

"I don't mean to scare you," she said. "But a man has been following you and staring at you. He started at the Coke machine. He's about fifteen feet behind you now. He's wearing a gray hat with a black band."

Did Altman have a hat?

"I just wanted to tell you," she said. "It happened to my sister and she—"

She choked up.

"That's okay," I said. "Thanks."

She walked away, gave me a tense look over her shoulder, and disappeared. I kept watching the juggler. He had switched to Indian clubs.

Altman wouldn't do anything funny out in public, I reassured myself. He's a very weird guy maybe, but not a psychopath. Right?

I pulled Lucas toward me, away from the candy bar wrapper he was licking, and pressed his head against my knees.

Besides, I've got a vicious three-legged dog with me.

He raised his muzzle. I backstroked the bristly fur underneath his chin and he rolled his eyes in ecstasy.

So why were my hands shaking?

Ordinarily, the languid motion of the Indian clubs would have been mesmerizing. Like a fire in a fireplace or clothes in a glass-front dryer. But right now I was unmesmerizable. I tried to slow my pulse to match the rhythm—slap and toss, slap and toss, slap and toss—but it didn't work.

"Libby!"

And again.

"Libby!"

I scanned the crowd to my left. Then a hand touched my right shoulder. I felt the way you do when you step into a hole you hadn't noticed: my heart leapt like a toad.

"Libby, " a man's voice said. "Your hair is different. I didn't recognize you at first."

I jerked around.

Who was this guy? He was tall and thin, with dark eyes and pale skin. He was wearing wrinkled khakis, a Hawaiian print shirt, a brown cardigan sweater with droopy pockets, and, like the lady said, a gray hat with a black band.

He was smiling. A little. Nervously.

Surely I knew him. He had that sort of once-removed look. Like he was somebody's brother.

He raised his hand to the brim of his hat. My eyes followed the hand, which looked peculiar. Missing fingers or something. I couldn't tell and didn't want to stare.

He took the hat off.

"Libby, it's me. Jack. Jack Hale."

Jesus. It was. It was his voice, anyway. And that was the hand that he blew up with a firecracker after college.

15

It was Jack Hale, except his hair had gone absolutely white since I'd last seen him, and he weighed about thirty pounds less than he used to.

Lucas pressed his head against Jack's shin.

"Of course. It's you. Jack. I can't believe it. I mean I guess I can. I know you live around here, but-"

He looked slacker than he had in the old days. He used to look—it was hard to say exactly what—fearless, I suppose. Fearless and frenetic and kind of wild. Now he looked more tentative. Dimmed, somehow. Like he couldn't move as fast as he used to.

Maybe we were all getting that way.

It was odd to see him without Andrea. Like seeing someone you know suddenly missing an eye.

I bit my lip but the tears came anyway.

"Jesus, Jack, I'm sorry—" My voice shocked me, it was so tight and low.

"—about Andrea. I think about her a lot. I think about her and—"

I fought hard against an urge to sit down on the sidewalk and sob.

I'd felt sad about Andrea before, but this was different. Like a riptide was pulling me. Was it thinking about Andrea that made me feel this way? Or was it seeing Jack?

"That's okay," he said. "I got your letter."

He reached down and petted Lucas.

"That was enough."

The couple standing to my right, catching sight of my tears, edged away. Maybe they thought Jack and I were having a fight.

Jack stepped closer to me.

"What are you doing here? Are you in for the weekend? You look kind of tired."

His voice was lots gentler than it used to be.

"What's wrong?" he said.

"It's okay," I said. "It was from thinking about Andrea. You know what I mean—"

Of course he did. His eyes were full, too.

My voice came back.

"Come on," I said. "Let's go for a walk."

We walked out of the Square, over the bridge, and along a cement footpath that bordered the Charles. We found a bench and sat down.

At first we avoided mentioning Andrea the way you'd avoid going near a power line that fell down in the street. I told Jack about the seminar I was teaching—about tomorrow's session on Margaret Bourke-White and Dorothea Lange. It was the kind of subject Jack used to get excited about. He'd been a fiend for Walker Evans once. Back when we were in school he could talk all evening without mentioning anything but photography. I remembered his apartment in Rochester: no furniture—just a sleeping bag, a stack of photography books, and whatever photographic contraption he was working on at the time.

"We have your book," he said. "The tap dancers. It's really good."

"Thanks." It still surprises me when someone who's not related to me has seen it.

"Andrea" he said, "was really pleased. It made her happy to see it. She talked about buying some of your pictures."

We stared at the river for a while, its surface streaked with reflected light from the bridge. Lucas fell asleep. A couple of guys in sweats started pitching a glow-in-the-dark Frisbee in the space between us and the water.

Jack leaned his head back on the bench and closed his eyes. I wondered if he was asleep, too.

I didn't want to close my eyes. I was afraid that if I did, the news coverage of the discovery of Andrea's body would play through my mind. The parking garage elevator. The sheet-covered lump on the stretcher. Her hand.

Jack was absolutely still. God, I thought. He was crazy about her. He'd been married to her, well, forever it seemed. What kind of pictures ran through his mind? How did he stop them?

His hands were resting on his thighs. I took a closer look at the right one. The pinky and ring finger were intact, but the middle finger was missing everything down to just below where the first knuckle should be.

I hadn't realized that the accident had been that bad.

Jack's left hand was against my right, the little arcs of hair grazing my skin. The layer of air between us felt warm and wired, like the air over the hood of your car when the engine is idling.

How old was I then? Nineteen? Twenty? It was the end of spring term my sophomore year; I was getting ready to leave for my summer job—waitressing at the Oprygrounds near Wheeling—and doing some last-minute darkroom work.

Jack was behind me. I was doing him a favor—trying out an enlarger he was working on. He was trying to make it lighter—collapsible maybe. Something like that. I was too busy to take the time for it, but he could talk you into anything, back then.

I knew him a little, from parties, from him hanging around the darkrooms trying to get people to try out his inventions. New filters. A voltage regulator. He was smart, sarcastic, and looked kind of like James Taylor with a better body. Andrea, who worked food service with me, told me she heard he had an American flag tattooed on his rear end.

Somebody in the next room was playing a radio

loud. *The Doors. The bass surged through the floorboards. Dark, seductive. The undertow.*

Jack reached forward to tighten a screw on the machine's neck; I adjusted the film in the holder. The safelight on the wall glowed through the fog of gray and black, dusting the light-colored things with amber—the countertops, my arms, his hands.

I burned the image into the paper, sank the paper into the developing tray.

It was a picture of the entrance to the greenhouse at the Brooklyn Botanical Gardens. The blocks that were the panes of whitewashed glass accumulated—slowly, silently—within their gray metal frames, like snow gathering on tree branches.

"Nice," Jack whispered against my neck. "Very nice."

He smelled like sweat and darkroom chemicals. Or was that me?

He was right. The picture was nice. Very nice. I warmed with satisfaction, lifted it out of the developing tray, rinsed it, and fixed it.

I felt him press me from behind, felt how hard he was against my rear end. I leaned backward into him and gently slid up and down, like a bear scratching her back on a tree.

He slipped his hands into my shirt—I was braless—I always was then—and pressed them against my chest.

It was the best sex I ever had. Maybe because the foreplay was printing pictures. Or maybe it was the tattoo. The safelight? Who knows.

We did it on the counter, on the floor, and against the door. It didn't matter how much sound we made because Jim Morrison was drowning us out. When I licked Jack he tasted like salt and darkroom chemicals. I probably have a brain lesion from it.

I left that night for Wheeling. When I got back to Rochester at the end of the summer I called him up, and Andrea answered the phone. She'd been living with him since July, she said. They were crazy in love.

So that was that. Afterward Jack and I always pretended it had never happened.

"Want to go to your place?"

"No," I said. That was for sure. I opened my mouth to tell him about Altman, then felt foolish.

"Somebody's there," I said. "How about yours?"

He was quiet for a while. The Frisbee landed near my foot. I whipped it back to the kids and waited for him to talk.

"I don't have a place right now," he said. "I'm living out at my mom's. She's not doing real great. She had hip replacement surgery and it got infected. She's walking but she's not real steady. I moved the shop out there, too. To the barn."

And it could be, I thought, that he didn't like being alone. After what happened.

"But," he said, "I've got keys to a friend's place. I've been watching it. Checking in on it. Watering the plants. Taking in the mail."

Keys to a friend's place? It sounded like college. But then I'd been obsessing about college all evening.

We walked to his car—a woody station wagon with the backseat yanked out to make more room for cargo.

I helped Lucas into the back, then sat down next to Jack. It was the kind of car you might find at the dump: the latch was missing from my seatbelt; dead, crumbling foam rubber leaked out of cracks in the upholstery; all that was left of the sun visor on my side was a metal rod.

I wondered what Andrea had thought of it.

5

THE CONDO WAS THE DOWNSTAIRS OF A TWO-FAMILY HOUSE, THE only modern building on a West Cambridge street lined with full-grown trees, beat-up Saabs, and nicely maintained Victorian houses painted in earth tones. While Jack fumbled with his keys I peered down the street, imagining the modest-size families inside the houses, eating complementary proteins while they watched public television.

He unlocked the door; I stepped over the upstairs neighbor's mail and newspapers, then followed Jack into the apartment. Lucas hung close to my legs, afraid of the dark and the strangeness. The place smelled stale and humid—the way a Thermos does when you haven't used it for a long time.

I pressed the switch for the front hall light. The bulb blew out, sending Lucas into a spasm of panic. In the flare I made out a few pieces of furniture covered with sheets—a table or desk maybe, with a plant on it; a chair; what might have been a rolled-up rug propped against a wall.

I found another switch. This one lit an enormous room to my left—the one Jack had disappeared into. A person writing for a home-decorating magazine would have called it "handsome"—the kind of place only white-collar criminals can afford in New York: satiny hardwood trim and floors, white walls, built-in bookcases, and subtle, expensive touches, like brass-capped electrical outlets sunk into the floor, wooden heating vents, and lamps mounted on the walls without any extra wires running out of them. A kitchen was at the far end, separated from the dining area by a sleek granite counter big enough to do heart surgery on. A door with stained glass panels stood ajar in an alcove partway down the living room wall; through it I could make out an antique porcelain pedestal sink.

It looked like someone was moving out. Or had started moving out and forgotten to go back for the rest. A stereo speaker lay on a tony-looking cream-colored couch; a couple of flattened U-Haul boxes leaned against its arm; an empty packing tape dispenser, bits of grit, and some dustballs had been swept into a mound in the center of the floor.

I crossed the room and opened the refrigerator, hoping for something cold to drink. It was empty except for an open box of baking soda tipped on its side.

What was that supposed to do? Keep the roaches out? I closed the door and leaned into the hallway.

"What's the story, Jack?" I yelled. "Did this guy have to skip the country or something?"

He didn't answer.

I found a bucket under the sink, filled it with water for Lucas, and went into the next room: a bedroom, as it turned out, with another light that didn't work. A narrow band of windows circled the room near the ceiling in a way that seemed very austere, very fifties. In the streetlight that sifted through the glass I could make out a sheetless double-bed mattress on the floor and a pot with a half-dead orchid plant in it.

Jack was in the bathroom.

I cranked a window open, closed the door because I don't like Lucas to see me in bed with somebody, and sat down on the mattress.

Jack came out of the bathroom and lay beside me, face-down.

The only movement in the room was the "Federal Law Prevents Removal of This Tag" tag on the mattress, trembling in the slight breeze. The only sounds were distant and outside: a branch of a pine tree brushing against the window screens; the plinking of a wind chime on somebody's porch; the occasional hum of tires on asphalt.

"So, Jack," I said. "Whose place is this? Why don't they get the rest of their stuff?"

He didn't answer.

I leaned closer to him.

His eyes were closed but I could tell from the tense way he held the muscles around his mouth that he wasn't asleep. He contorted his face slightly, as though he were about to say something, then stopped. Something glimmered on his skin. A tear? I reached out to make sure.

His cheek was slick with them. They were running in a silent stream from the corner of his eye and collecting in the hair at his temple.

Silent, manly crying. Why don't they just convulse like the rest of us?

A wheel of sadness turned inside my chest. I didn't know whether it was a good idea to hug him—whether it would make things better or worse. I settled for touching my hand to his elbow.

23

"I shouldn't have come here with you," I said. "I'm sorry."

I was trying to speak in ordinary tones, but the words came out in a whisper.

"I make you think about Andrea. About when we were kids. You know, that's what we were, practically. Back then."

He didn't say anything.

I lay down and watched the shadows of the tree branches skim the ceiling. They were thick and slow and ropey-looking, like plants swaying below the surface of a lake. They made me feel slow, too. Tired and slow.

"I can't stop thinking about her either, Jack. She was the smartest person I ever knew. She wouldn't—"

That wasn't it. Not just smart, even though she was. Explosively. Glowingly.

"No. She was—"

What? Sensitive? Compassionate? The words seemed pale.

"I don't know, Jack. Maybe it was that she always knew what was important better than anybody I've ever known. Like when her parents died. Remember how crazy everybody thought she was for leaving RIT? For taking care of her brother the way she did? People said she was making a martyr out of herself. I said it, too. But she knew it was the right decision—for her. You must have, too. You stuck with her, Jack. You stuck with her through everything."

Not like me, I thought, flushing with guilt.

Not like me.

I could remember the last time I'd talked with Andrea; more than ten years ago—a couple of years after I'd moved to New York.

She'd called me. She'd said she was sorry it had been so long since we'd been in touch, but things had been hectic. She was about to finish law school; she was writing a chapter for a legal textbook; she had a job lined up for the fall. Things like that.

She and Jack had gotten married, she told me.

I remember sitting down when she told me that. On the indoor-outdoor carpet that was glued to my apartment's concrete floor.

City Hall, she'd said. Nothing fancy.

And by the way—they were renting a place on Cape Cod for a while. It had an extra room—did I want to come visit?

Thanks Andrea, I'd said. Sounds nice. I'll let you know.

And I never did. Never called, never wrote. Nothing.

Where was my life headed then? I was living in a subbasement studio on Sixteenth Street that a neighbor told me two women had been murdered in a year earlier; I was a messenger for the magazine I was desperate to take photographs for; and I'd just found out that a guy I'd had a crush on for months was gay.

Those were the days.

I should have called her back. I should have sent a present. I shouldn't have been jealous.

Jack went back to the bathroom. Through the grayness I watched him guzzle water from the faucet, then wipe his face on the shower curtain liner that hung half in, half out of the tub. He came back and lay down again, this time on his back.

"This was your place, Jack, wasn't it? Yours and Andrea's. Your bed, too."

I'd probably known it from the moment we'd walked in the door. From the way he'd walked so confidently through the dark rooms. From the way he'd gone straight for the bathroom off the big bedroom instead of the guest bath off the hall.

He still didn't say anything.

"Why did you bring me here? It doesn't look like you live here anymore. Why didn't you bring me somewhere else?"

He rubbed the palms of his hands from the front to the

25

back of his hair. The gesture reminded me of something. Someone. I couldn't remember.

"I told you," he said. "I don't have a place anymore. I'm living out at my mom's. In the barn."

Lucas was clawing at the door. I got up and let him in. He went into the bathroom, turned around a few times, and lay down on the ceramic tile floor. I sat on the mattress again, leaning my back against the wall where the headboard should have been. It had been a long time since I'd sat around in the dark with a guy I barely knew. If I'd been eighteen I would have lit up a joint.

"When was the last time you were here?"

"I don't know," he said. "Sometime after the cops finished going through it."

Something had grown odd about the timing of his responses. There was a slightly longer delay than seemed right. Like the conversations the cab driver has with the dispatcher on the radio, where they have to take the time to press a button in order to talk.

"Did you have to talk to them a lot? What are they doing? Aren't they still investigating this?"

This time there was more than a pause.

"They say they are," he finally said. "But I've stopped wanting to ask questions."

I imagined the detectives here, in this room. Going through the pockets of Andrea's clothes that hung in the closet, looking for address books, calendars, diaries, checking the labels on the prescription pills.

"They were even after me, you know," he said.

His voice had gone tight, angry.

"Like I would kill her, or hire somebody to. Who could dream something like that up? They found out my partner had moved in with me out at the lab and figured we were getting it on or something. I don't know. It still seems like it

couldn't have happened. That I watched it happen to someone else."

"Your partner?"

"Sammy Clay. You never met him."

"No. What's he like?"

"We've been working on a camera together. Compact. With
a flexible neck. Architects love it. You can work it into design
models and take photographs inside of them. It's got a million applications. Sam calls it the Snake Eye. He's good at
that part of the business. Marketing. Getting distribution.
That end."

"So why did Sammy move in with you?"

He did the nervous thing with the palms of his hands
against his hair again. Now I remembered why it looked
familiar: Max does the same thing.

When he's making things up.

"He split up with his wife," he said. "Or she split up with
him. Nobody's filed for divorce yet, but they will. It's a bad
situation. They've got little kids. At first he just wanted to
crash for a couple of nights, but now—"

"It's more like forever?"

I remembered Altman and my stomach contracted.

"It's okay," he said. "He's under a lot of stress. Needs someone to talk to. Plus we get a lot of work done."

"Sure," I said. It sounded more like a misery-loves-com-
pany situation to me than anything else, but if it made them
comfortable—

"We were working together," he said, "the day Andrea was
killed."

He said the "was killed" part more loudly, more clearly,
than the other words, as though he'd had to train himself to
use the phrase without falling apart.

"You don't have to talk about it anymore," I said. "I understand."

And I did. I can still get choked up about my mother and my brother from the smallest things—like seeing someone with the kind of pocketbook she used to have, or hearing a little of the music that Avery used to like, or . . .

"I want to, Libby," he said. "I have to. Otherwise it just overloads my mind. If I didn't talk to you I'd be talking to myself. I brought you here because I can't stand to come here alone. The last time I was here one of the cops came in and tried to get me to tell him that Andrea was having an affair with Mark LeClair."

"Isn't that what a lot of people think?"

The tears started again.

"He showed me a copy of the note they say they found in her bag in the courtroom."

"I read about it. What did it say?"

"'Pokey,'" he said.

He drew absently in the air with his finger while he remembered the words.

"It said 'Pokey, I love you. But I'm not ready. I may never be.'"

"'Pokey?'"

"Yeah. 'Pokey.'"

"Was it in her handwriting?"

"It looked like her handwriting."

"So the police think she had a pet name for LeClair: Pokey."

"That's right. They claimed they had somebody who heard her call him that on the phone once."

"Who?"

"They wouldn't say."

"If they're so sure that he duped her into falling in love with him and helping him escape and then killed her, why were they going for you?"

"I don't know."

"Did you ever hear her call anybody Pokey? Did she ever have a pet name for you?"

"Me? She called me Jack. That's all."

"Did she ever talk to you about this guy—LeClair?"

A car pulled into the driveway of the next house, the radio tuned loud to a rock station. The driver turned it off and slammed the door. Jack waited until the footsteps receded before he spoke, as though someone that far away could hear him.

"Talk about him? She hated him. She used to call me every time she finished a meeting with him. She said he was the first person who ever made her believe that the devil existed. You know how she was: she always gave everybody the benefit of the doubt. Think how she was with her brother. The kid practically robbed her blind, but she was always back for more—"

"How's he taking this?"

He shrugged.

"I don't know. Okay, I guess. He seems to be staying clean, anyway. I don't talk to him much."

"It must be hard for him."

He didn't respond.

He was lying on his stomach again, his face turned away from me. I thought he'd fallen asleep. I started to slip, too.

Then suddenly his breathing turned shallow and sharp and irregular, like an old person's. I put my hand on his shoulder.

"Jack, what's the matter? Is that asthma? Do you need me to get you something?"

I went to the bathroom, filled an abandoned Dunkin' Donuts coffee cup with water, and crouched on the floor by his head.

He sat up just as I extended the cup to him, accidentally knocking it out of my hand. The panel of light that glowed from the partially open bathroom door blanched his face; his eyes looked frightened.

"It's true," he said. "I saw her."

"Who?"

"Andrea."

"When? What do you mean?"

Lucas picked up on the alarmed sound in my voice and trotted over to the bed, eyeing Jack warily.

"On a bus," he said. "Coming out of the Harvard Square underpass."

"When?" I repeated. "What are you talking about?"

"A month ago," he said. "I was crossing Mount Auburn Street, going to the post office. I looked up and there she was, looking out the window."

Lucas whimpered and pawed at the mattress.

My heart was slamming against my ribs like someone banging on the door to tell you the house is on fire. Was he absolutely nuts?

"You've got to believe me," he said. "It was her. She was wearing the sweater I gave her for her birthday. I paid Sammy's wife to knit it for her. I could only see her from the chest up, but it was Andrea, Lib, in the sweater. It was that green color Andrea liked. Light green. What did she call it? She always liked the fancy words for colors."

He closed his eyes.

"Celadon," he said. "That was the color: celadon."

Then he stood up and crossed the room to the doorway. His gait seemed a little awkward—like the muscular equivalent of the speech delay. And something about the way the shadows worked in the room made him seem taller and even more attenuated than he really was.

"You were right," he said. "This was a mistake. I can't stay here anymore."

He reached into his pocket, wrenched a key from his key

chain, and tossed it toward the mattress. It stung me on the leg.

I flinched.

Lucas tensed and raised his head.

"Keep it," Jack said.

He left before I could answer.

6

I woke up shivering, confused about why I still had my jeans on and where I was. The sun was barely up.

Good thing, I thought, tugging at my shirt, which had wound itself straitjacket fashion around me while I slept. I was supposed to teach at eight. That gave me less than an hour and a half to pick up my lecture notes, dress in something that connoted a little authority, and get to school.

Lucas was in the bathroom. His muzzle was stuck in the Dunkin' Donuts cup I'd filled for Jack the night before, and he was trying to extricate himself by rubbing it against the door frame.

I pulled it off his snout.

"And you, poor babe," I told him, "we've got to run back home and get you your Purina. If Altman hasn't eaten it, that is."

Last night's warm weather had been freakish; this morning

it was November-as-usual. The floor was like ice and nothing was coming out of the heating vents. I'd had the sense to crank the window shut before I'd fallen asleep, but still the room felt like the dairy section at D'Agostino's.

Jack had left his watch on the floor next to the mattress. I pocketed it and opened the closet door, hoping I'd find a jacket or sweater. The closet had been cleaned out except for an empty shoe box and a torn brown shopping bag with MORGAN MEMORIAL scrawled on it in pencil. Inside the bag were two pairs of Levi's, both with the knees worn through, a chlorine-damaged bathing suit, and a navy blue sweatshirt with a rip in the arm. Lucas sniffed at the pile, impressed with the dank old clothes smell.

"Nice, huh boy? The clothes people think poor folks will want to wear?"

I wondered who had sorted through Andrea's clothes, who had filled the bag. Jack? Somebody from Andrea's work? Her brother?

I pulled on the sweatshirt, reached into the hand-warmer pocket, and pulled out some trash. An empty book of matches, a paper wrapper from a drinking straw, a crumpled Kleenex, and a small piece of paper folded in half and in half again. I smoothed it open on my knee.

The handwriting was Andrea's. I remembered it very well: firm, clear, with up-and-down strokes. I used to compare her class notes to mine and feel inadequate. But the notepaper, torn off a pad so there was a gummy ridge at the top, with a picture of a girl walking barefoot on the beach, her footprints trailing behind, didn't look like anything Andrea would have owned. And what the hell was she writing about?

> *I like sunsets, strangers, sick jokes,*
> *Sour apples.*
> *Long walks, my Walkman, mountaintop views,*

Short nails, Chapstick, Teva sandals,
Barbara Kingsolver, all shades of green,
The way you walk, the crinkles around your eyes
when you laugh . . .
What about you?

"Andrea," I said out loud. "What *is* this?"

The note—or was it a poem?—was adolescent-sounding, Rod McKuenish even—like something you would pass to a crush in high school study hall. I read it one more time, stuffed it in my wallet, and hightailed it out of the apartment with Lucas. We waited for the light on Huron, then broke into a jog.

"Well, buddy," I told him. "I guess we should be glad we found that thing, and not just anybody."

And who in the world was it meant for?

My Rabbit was still at the curb in front of Altman's. So were my clothes, film, lights, duffel bag, shampoo, boxes of slides, and binders of lecture notes.

I tried the front door, but it was chained from the inside. Lucas squeezed his nose into the crack.

"Sorry," I told him. "I guess we're not home quite yet."

A page from Altman's prescription pad was taped to the duffel with a Band-Aid. I ripped it from the canvas.

"Dear friend," it said. "I'm sorry you were unhappy with our arrangement. I'm afraid it simply wasn't meant to be."

I loaded the stuff into my car. The Cambridge Visitor Parking Permit that Altman had loaned me was still on the dashboard.

A bargaining chip, I thought. Not bad.

7

THE SEMINAR WENT OKAY. THAT IS, THE SLIDE PROJECTOR WORKED, a couple of the kids were more interested in discussing the topic than in taking notes, and Lucas didn't pee on the floor, like he did the first day.

Today's subject was "Recording the Depression: Selected Photographers of the Thirties."

I was contrasting Margaret Bourke-White's and Dorothea Lange's dust bowl pictures, especially the photographs they took of tenant farmers' homes. When Bourke-White took her WPA pictures, she did things like rearrange the items on the dresser and tell people where to sit. Lange, as far as anybody knows, did no such thing, and conventional criticism has it that she was the more "honest," and therefore the "better" photographer. The class sniffed in disapproval when I talked about Bourke-White and brightened when I brought up Lange.

But didn't Lange, I asked them, by photographing a woman

from an angle that would include, say, a broken-down truck, not necessarily the subject's, in the background, also manipulate the image and the audience? Isn't photography by its nature manipulative because the image is defined by the frame of the viewfinder and the moment the shutter is released?

The couple of students who talked really ran with it. One of them brought up the famous Robert Doisneau photograph of Parisian lovers that until recently everybody assumed was one of those once-in-a-lifetime, magic-of-the moment shots. Now, half a century later, a man and a woman had identified themselves as the couple Doisneau had paid to pose for the picture.

Does the photographer owe us an apology?

Should art be moral? Can it be?

The conversation reminded me of conversations I'd had with Jack back when he was the only other person I knew who really thought about things like that. Back when he talked.

I thought about the look on his face the night before when he'd talked about Andrea. About the way he seemed to disappear emotionally sometimes. What was wrong with him?

Class dismissed.

Nobody hung around afterward to talk like they usually do, except for the guy in the necktie who always wanted to help me with things. Like wind the cord around the projector. Make sure the slides were right-side-up in the box. Get me coffee. If I'd used an overhead projector he would have wanted to lick the transparencies clean. And what was wrong with him?

I called Jack from my office and told him I had his watch. Now he sounded cheerful and clear-headed.

"You know what they say, Libby, about women who leave things behind in guys' apartments—"

"That it means they want to come back?"

I didn't point out that the analogy was off-key—that it wasn't my apartment he'd left the watch in.

"Why don't you bring it out here and have a sandwich or something? You can take a look at Argus."

What was that? His dog?

"I can show you around. You can try out the Snake Eye if you want."

Of course, Argus was the company in the barn.

I wrote down the directions he gave me in the margin of my *Boston Street Atlas*, then looked up Altman's office number in the phone book. I was kicking myself for not having gotten a written lease from him. When I'd asked him about it, way back in September, he'd been incredulous.

"For four months?" he had asked, as though I had asked him to do a blood-brother ceremony with me. "Why would we need a lease for such a short time? I prefer a relationship based on trust, don't you?"

Yeah, I guess so.

"Ronnie?"

"This is Dr. Altman."

"Ronnie, this is Libby Kincaid. I want back in my apartment this afternoon. And I don't want you to be there."

"As I told you, Libby, it's not that I don't want you in the apartment, it's just that I think we could coexist peacefully there. In fact, if you want to invite a friend, or a colleague—"

"I'm entitled to this apartment, Ronnie."

His white-noise sound-deflecting machine was purring in the background.

"Then I suggest," he said, "that you bring the matter up with your lawyer."

What lawyer? The only lawyers I knew were in New York, and I was still trying to pay their gigantic bills.

"Sure, Ronnie," I said. "I'll do that."

Driving to Boston's western suburbs from Cambridge is like watching slow-motion footage of a tornado. The houses drift farther and farther apart, the trees come closer and closer together, the lawn ornaments thin, then disappear, disappear, disappear altogether . . . .

Turn left off Trapelo at the flowerpot.

This had to be it. Not that the town had a sign that said "The Kiwaniqueens Welcome You to Lincoln" at the border or anything. Not that it had street signs, even. Just a couple of massive white pre–Revolutionary War houses, a town library, and a lot of nature.

Right at Codman Farm.

Cows. A barn. A dirt parking lot with six kinds of Volvos in it and a sign that said COMMUNITY GARDENS.

This was confusing. What do people who have three-acre zoning need community gardens for?

I swerved to avoid a man on a bicycle dragging a little kid behind him in a thing that looked like a plastic rickshaw.

"Jesus," I hissed, my heart somewhere near my tonsils. "Somebody ought to report that guy to the state. Put that poor baby in foster care."

Stone walls, big trees, amber waves of grain.

Left after the Unitarian Church.

It was a dirt road, full of holes, with a hand-carved wooden sign at the entrance that said PRIVATE ROAD. RESIDENTS ONLY. Tasteful yet intimidating.

Another way the people out here are different from you and me is that they have no street numbers, at least not where anybody could see them. Mailboxes, yes; newspaper boxes, yes. But no hints about who lives where.

Wasn't that the reason Herman Tarnower bled to death? Because his neighborhood was so exclusive the paramedics couldn't find his house?

Now and then I caught a glimpse of a tennis court or a stable through the woods; the houses were too far back to see.

Last driveway before the dead end.

Driveway, no. A practice slope for an Olympic freestyle skiing team, yes. I drove with the brakes on, churning gravel and dirt on both sides, and made it down the hill. The drive leveled out through the woods for a while, curved sharply, then dropped again.

Straight ahead was an enormous field of dead corn; to the right a sprawling, gloomy combination of farmhouse and Adirondack lodge, with a stone foundation and dark screened-in porches on two sides; to the left, where the drive ended, stood a brown barn with a solar collector on the roof. As I drove toward the building an older woman, her gray hair wound into knots over both ears, limped out from behind the farmhouse, shielded her eyes, and stared at Lucas and me. She was wearing a down vest over a yellow-and-white seersucker dress that had a zipper down the front, heavy brown shoes, and white cotton anklets. Everything looked as though it didn't quite fit; like she'd bought it all mail order but didn't want to spend the postage to send it back and get the right size.

Jack walked out the barn door as I switched off the engine. He nodded, then turned around and walked back in. I let Lucas out of the car and followed.

"It's kind of remote out here," I said. "I guess you don't get a whole lot of Jehovah's Witnesses."

If he heard me he didn't let me know. He sat down on a stool at a twenty-foot-long table—the kind people use at church picnics—frowning at a piece of metal. His mouth was so tense his lips had almost disappeared. I decided he was in

39

the middle of something, shut up, and scanned the barn.

The room was halfway remodeled, as though Jack had started the job and gotten tired, or distracted by the inventing, or maybe didn't have the heart for it after Andrea was killed. Leftover lumber from the new floor lay stacked against the back wall. One side of the barn had huge windows, but faded, curling installation and care instructions were still taped to them, obscuring the view. The plaster walls were dirty and covered with smeared penciled instructions for the placement of outlets, lights, and shelves that hadn't yet gone in or weren't going to.

There was a soapstone sink—one of the only items left from the original barn, it seemed—near the front door. I poured some water into a jar for Lucas and helped him guzzle it. Then I sat down on one of the stools and looked out the window.

The woman I'd waved to outside was dragging a metal bucket into the field. When she got to about the center, she turned the bucket upside down, straddled it, and started hacking at the ground with a big iron tool—something like a crowbar with a pointed foot at the end of it.

Now that I could see her profile I was sure the woman was Jack's mom; she had the same high-bridged nose, the same wide forehead, the same intense expression while she worked. Her legs were thin and her shoulders were rounded, but her grandmotherly appearance belied her strength. She was landing wallops on the ground that sent rocks and clumps of dirt sailing five feet in the air around her, making a thudding sound that reached to the barn.

I lifted my camera to my eye, then lowered it. No way I'd get anything but a cloud of dirt.

I turned to Jack. He was trying successively smaller screwdrivers on a screw in a joint on the piece of metal.

I put his watch on the table next to him. He grunted, dropped it into his shirt pocket, and kept working.

"What's that thing your mother's swinging out there? She's amazing with it."

He picked up a wire, and, one eye closed, inserted it into the joint. It was impressive, really, how well his injured hand worked.

"The mattock?" he said. "It's kind of funny, isn't it? She used to move plants around all the time. Now I think she just likes swinging something. I've told her she ought to take up golf instead."

I tried to imagine her on the fairway, in crisp culottes, a visor, and spiked shoes, like the women you see in the sports section.

No way.

Lizzie Borden was more like it.

My stomach growled. I looked around for the promised sandwich, but didn't see anything like food. Just tools and eviscerated cameras.

"Hey Jack," I said. "Why don't you finish up what you're doing while I go out to the deli and get us some lunch?"

As soon as the words came out I realized they were stupid. No delis out here. Probably no pop machine at the gas station, either. Unless it was made out of granite or something, with the Coca-Cola trademark carved into it.

Jack gave a final twist to whatever he was doing, gave a barely perceptible satisfied nod of his head, and walked to the far end of the barn, where the lumber was. I followed. In one corner there was a folding wooden cot, like the ones evacuees sleep on in VFW halls during a hurricane. On top of the cot there was an ancient sleeping bag from before they started coming in mummy shapes, with a lip of red plaid lining showing at the top. Next to the cot were two orange crates full of books—*A Brief History of Time* was one of them—and a reading lamp.

I was about to make a crack about the setup looking like solitary confinement when I noticed a second wooden cot directly across the room. This one was made up with a sheet and a brown blanket—tight, with mitered corners, like a box gift-wrapped at the store.

Jack followed my gaze.

"That's my partner's," he said. "Sammy's. I told you about him."

He reached under the sleeping bag–bed and pulled out a circular tin box with a picture of poinsettias on the lid, two red plastic cups, and a jar, like an old pickle jar, filled with a clear liquid.

He walked back to the table and spread a newspaper at one end of it. Then he opened up the tin, peeled off a layer of highly recycled aluminum foil, and took out four sandwiches, each one wrapped in wax paper as neatly as the second cot was wrapped in its blanket.

He handed two of the sandwiches to me and took two for himself.

We unwrapped them.

They were weird. It looked like whoever had made them had bought presliced bread and cut the pieces in half again, so they were about an eighth of an inch thick. Inside each sandwich half was a tough piece of yellow cheese about the size of a credit card. No mustard. No mayo.

Jack bit into his, took the lid off the beverage jar, and handed me my cup. It had screw threads inside the rim, like a lid from a busted Thermos.

This would explain why he looked so much thinner than he used to.

"Jack," I said. "What's with the sandwiches? Are you on a diet or something?"

He looked surprised. Then he looked embarrassed.

"Do you mean the bread?"

"Right. The bread. And the cheese, too."

"My mother makes them this way. She thinks it saves money. I don't even notice it anymore. Here's what you do—"

He stacked two sandwiches, making something almost normal-size.

"See? Same difference."

I gulped the juice. I didn't say anything, but I was pretty sure it was leftover from cans of mandarin orange sections.

"Your mother fixes your food?"

At school Jack had seemed to me like someone who didn't have parents at all, just grew inside a peach or something like the boy in the Japanese fairy tale. The idea of his mother filling the round tin box for him every morning stunned me. Was this really the same guy who used to lie down at night on the airstrip at Rochester Airport and watch the planes take off over him?

"She started to do it after I moved back."

"Last year?"

"Yeah. Last year."

The frown on his face deepened.

"You don't understand, Libby. I was a mess. I could hardly drive a car. Andrea dying. The investigation. It was . . . "

His voice got slow again, the way it had the night before when he started talking about Andrea.

"And then she got sick, so I thought, 'if it makes her happy to keep on doing this—fixing my food, doing my laundry— why don't I let her . . . '"

And then you got used to it, I figured. Besides, he was swamping himself in his work so he didn't have to think about Andrea, and he didn't care what he was eating. I once lived for a month on blue Popsicles and yogurt.

"We talked about Robert Doisneau today," I said. "At

school. The integrity question. A couple of them really dove in. You would have . . . "

His face was blank.

I stopped talking and he didn't notice.

So much for my fantasy about sizzling intellectual conversation. Had I been remembering right? Did he really used to talk about these things?

The phone rang. While Jack crossed the room to answer it I handed one of my sandwiches under the table to Lucas. I had Pop-Tarts out in the glove compartment. I could heat them up on the manifold while I drove back to Cambridge.

The caller was doing most of the talking, and whatever he or she was saying was making Jack happy. He smiled and tapped his fingers on the tabletop. Now and then he said "Okay!" or "Right!" His eyes looked clearer. His lips were back.

When he hung up he made a whooping sound, like "wooeee!"—the same sound he used to make when he was getting a party going.

The yell was infectious. Lucas let out a howl and I started to laugh.

"Jack—what's the deal? Who was that?"

He high-fived me so hard it stung.

"The Japanese!" he said. "Sammy made a deal with the Japanese! Everybody—the bank, Andrea, goddamit—even *I* told him he'd never pull it off and he did! Okay Sammy!"

He whooped again.

"Where is he?"

"Who?"

"Sammy."

"Down the road," he said. "He was calling from the car. He's coming out here to unload his stuff, to show me the deal."

A minute later a car, one of those low-slung ones with eyelids on the headlights, pulled up the drive and parked next to my Rabbit. A sandy-haired, pink-cheeked guy wearing aviator sunglasses, his necktie tossed over one shoulder, a briefcase in one hand, leapt out and hollered a greeting to Jack's mom. She turned in his direction, nodded slightly, and continued thwacking the ground.

He flung open the barn door and stood in the entrance, grinning. Lucas roused himself from his nap, growled half-heartedly, and closed his eyes again.

"So Jack," he yelled. "What did you do, buy another piece-of-shit car? You can place your order for a Porsche now, buddy—we're rich!"

"The piece-of-shit car, buddy," I said, "is mine. Or didn't you notice the New York plates?"

His pink cheeks turned red; his smile disappeared.

"Sorry," he said. "I didn't mean—"

He took his sunglasses off.

"I mean, I didn't see—"

Jack got up from his stool.

"Hey, lay off him, Lib! We're celebrating!"

He wiped his hands on his pants and gave Sammy one of those quick, man-to-man hugs: firm, mechanical, lasting a second, maybe.

"So where's the deal, Sammy? Where's the purchase order? I need to see it. I want to frame it. Hand it over!"

Jack was beaming like a little kid. He was moving faster, his voice was strong; for a moment I thought he was the old Jack.

Sammy took some papers out of his briefcase and straightened them into piles.

"There?" Jack asked, reaching for a pile. "Is it in there?"

Sammy snatched it back and nodded toward me.

45

"Who is she, anyway, Jack? Is it okay to—?"

"Her?" He looked at me. "Hell yeah. That's Libby. She can hear this stuff."

Sammy tucked the papers back into the case.

"I don't know, Jack. This is sensitive. If she—"

"Show me the purchase order!"

Sammy cringed; Lucas barked. I kept quiet even though it burned me up to hear them talk about me in the third person.

Sammy closed the briefcase and balanced it on his lap.

"You got any beer in here, Jack?"

"No."

Sammy stared at the briefcase; Jack stared at Sammy. Jack's mother started up with her mattock again.

"It's coming, Jack, honest. They just need to run the language by the CEO. You know the Japanese, Jack. They're not like us. It takes time. You know that. But we made the deal, Jack. Honest. We shook hands on it. And you know the Japanese, Jack. They don't go back on their word. They—"

Jack had balled his hand into a fist.

"Nice dog," Sammy said to me, motioning toward Lucas. "You from around here?"

"No, I—"

Jack shook his head.

"You didn't get the deal."

Sammy ignored him.

"Rabbit's really a pretty good car," he said to me. "Andrea's brother, Patrick, had one. You know him?"

"I know about him," I said, "from Andrea. I never met him."

He narrowed his eyes. "You knew her? Andrea?"

"Yes," I said. "I knew Andrea from—"

He didn't wait for an answer, just wheeled back to Jack,

who was sitting on his stool with his arms folded across his chest, his right hand still in a fist.

"Hey Jack," Sammy said. "Get a load of this. I saw Patrick in Harvard Square this morning. He's got a new pickup. He says he's getting the landscape business going down on the Cape. He's got a couple of big clients—office parks. He looked good, Jack. He said to say hi. He said—"

Jack pulled on a sweatshirt.

"Excuse me, Lib," he said. "I've gotta go for a walk. You know how it is."

I watched him cross the field, stop and talk to his mother, then disappear on a trail that seemed to lead into the woods.

"Call of nature," Sammy said.

He ripped open an envelope that was on the table.

"I don't think so," I said. "He was really upset. Did you really not get this deal?"

He didn't answer.

When he finished reading whatever was in the envelope he dumped it in the trash, then stared out the window at the place where Jack had disappeared. All the cockiness had gone out of his posture; he looked as worn out as Jack. He chewed his nails for a while, stared some more, then sighed.

"You married?" he asked.

"No."

"Ever been?"

"No."

He sighed again. This time it had a shudder in it. I remembered sighing like that when I was kid.

"I got served papers today," he said. "My wife filed for divorce."

"No kidding."

"I knew it was coming," he said. "It wasn't a surprise or anything."

47

He shoved the briefcase under the table.

"And I think I might have fucked up this deal," he said. "Kind of bad."

The sun was starting to go down; a row of tall, narrowly branched trees cast barred shadows across the section of the field that Jack's mother stood in.

Sammy stared at his cot.

"I think I need a nap," he said. "Mind if I—"

Lucas started fidgeting near the door, ready to go.

"That might not be a bad idea," I said. "Not a bad idea at all."

8

THAT NIGHT, BY PHONE, JACK AND I AGREED THAT I'D STAY AT THE condo until the end of the term, getting rid of the supermarket discount fliers that came every day, checking for leaks in the ceiling, making it look like somebody lived there. He told me he didn't think he could ever go back again. The night he'd been there with me had unnerved him, he said. I asked him why he even bothered keeping it, why he didn't sell the place or hire somebody else to check on it. He was quiet for a long time.

"It's the plants, Lib," he said. "They were Andrea's. My mom hates houseplants; she won't have them out here. And—" His voice broke.

"And what, Jack?"

"And it was the last thing Andrea asked me to do. Before she died. She was staying at the office late during the trial, getting up while it was still dark. She asked me to take care of the plants. So I've been trying to do it, Lib. But it's too hard."

I didn't tell him that I was sure Andrea wouldn't have expected the obligation to last in perpetuity. Grief does funny things to people. Maybe he thought that as long as the plants were still alive and waiting for her in the condo, Andrea would somehow be alive, too.

"Her things are gone, Libby," he went on, "but it's almost like I can smell her there. Don't you know what I mean?"

I nearly left after the first couple of days.

For me it wasn't Andrea's scent, but certain things—a belt hanging out of sight in the back of the closet, an earring back wedged in a crack in the bathroom windowsill, a slight smudge of lipstick on the wall near a light switch—that sometimes made it feel as though she were there. Made me catch my breath and jerk my head around, sure I'd find her watching me.

But the neighborhood around Fayerweather Street was pleasant—the gray-haired couple whose bumper sticker said VISUALIZE WORLD PEACE asked me lots of friendly questions about Lucas and my teaching, there was good pizza and a funky antique shop on Huron Avenue, and we were lots closer to the reservoir than we'd been at Altman's.

So Thursday after class I did a homemade exorcism: moved the mattress across the bedroom floor, put my own clothes in the closet, hung up some photographic posters I'd bought at the Harvard Coop—Lisette Model's famous shot of the fat lady bending over in her bathing suit at the beach; a vase of dying Robert Mapplethorpe flowers; Edward Steichen's Flatiron Building in the drizzle to remind me of home. I got the Magic Broom out of the front-hall closet and ran it over the floors, Cometed the sinks, washed the refrigerator door, and wiped down the bathroom mirror.

I watered the plants, too. The jade was dry, so I soaked it; the leaves were growing droopy on one side, so I spun the pot around. The gloxinia on the front-hall table was starting to bloom. I watered it, then turned my attention to the orchid in the bedroom that looked nearly dead. Lucas followed, trying to convince me to take him out.

"You know what we need around here, buddy? A prayer plant. Or maybe we ought to try visualization. Here we go. Close your eyes. Sap is running through this sucker's veins. The orchid is blooming."

But I couldn't make anything come into my mind's eye except the orchid as it was: two brown sticks poking out of a pot, about as alive as a couple of coat hangers. Too bad, I thought, I don't know what color the flowers are supposed to be. Maybe that would help.

"You know what Andrea would have said about this plant, Lucas? She would have said pitch it and Jack knows it."

Lucas ran toward the front door, looking for his leash. I ran a Handi Wipe along the mantel.

There was a dripping sound. I spun around, looking for Lucas—

"Hold on, sweetie—I'll get you out!"

Except it wasn't Lucas.

I had overwatered the gloxinia. There was a pool on the front hall table around the pot, and water was spilling down the back leg. I yanked the table away from the wall to keep the dripping away from the wallpaper, then ran to the bathroom for towels.

Damn, I thought. *I could have wrecked this wood but good.*

I ran a towel along the top of the table. Then I pulled out the empty drawer and set it on the floor. Water had pooled in it, too. I rolled up a towel and pressed it against the back seam. Then I reached inside the drawer frame and dabbed at it with another towel.

The cloth snagged on something loose and dry feeling. Something that wasn't wood.

I ran my fingers inside along the raw wood, then got on my knees and peered in. A manila envelope, nine-by-twelve size, was attached to the bottom of the table. Very neatly, with a strip of masking tape along each edge, so that there was no chance the drawer action would dislodge the paper.

I peeled the tape from the wood.

So maybe it's the operating instructions. Maybe the warranty.

For a front-hall table?

The name of the firm that Andrea used to be with, Darling and Ueland, was printed at the top. Then "100 Franklin Place, Boston," and below that "Interoffice Mail" with lots of empty lines headed "To" and "From."

I unfastened the clasp, walked toward the window, and pulled out the contents.

Photographs. Black-and-white.

I opened the window shade for better light and straightened the prints.

The top one was of a woman sitting at a dressing table, her back to the mirror—the round kind with Ping-Pong ball lights around it, half of them dead, one of them broken. Her eyes were far apart, the lids half-closed with the weight of their false lashes. Her hair was black and dry-looking, like an old Barbie doll's, and ratted high on her head.

She was huge-bosomed, wide-waisted, and wore a G-string that cut into the flesh of her upper thighs. Rhinestone-encrusted disks clung to her nipples like far-out barnacles, tassels dripping from the centers. Her breasts, her arms, her belly shone with sweat, as though she'd just been exerting herself.

The woman held an unlit cigarette, and she was smiling

casually into the camera, as though the photographer were no stranger. Or maybe the look was part of the job.

Her pocketbook, big and white with slotted compartments, was open on the dressing table next to a jumble of lipsticks, combs, lotions, and a quart container of orange Fanta. A lidless can of hairspray poked out of it.

She was thirty-five, maybe older, maybe nice-looking under the makeup.

I slipped the picture to the back of the pile.

The rest were of the same woman as she dressed to go home. First one with her jeans on. Then one with her jeans and a sweatshirt on—the kind with the neckline intentionally ripped open. Then one where she was in the jeans and sweatshirt and bent over, fastening her sandals. They were white with seashells glued in the shape of a flower on the delta of vinyl that separated her big toe from the rest.

A striptease in reverse.

They were nice images, but sloppily printed. The contrast was off and no one had spotted them—that is, no one had bothered to paint over the white specks that show up when dust gets on the negative.

There was no writing on the envelope, and none on the backs of the prints. The envelope held nothing but the photographs: no note, no receipt.

Andrea and Jack had cleaners, I told myself. Or somebody here doing a lot of work on the building. Maybe a worker stashed them here so his wife wouldn't find them at home. He found the Darling and Ueland envelope here in the trash. Or—

"Jack will know," I said, half to Lucas, half to myself.

I felt uncomfortable.

What if the pictures belonged to Jack? What if the woman had been Jack's girlfriend? Still was?

Hell, I thought. He would have taken the envelope away by now. He wouldn't have wanted the cops to find something like that, not if they'd been trying to implicate him in Andrea's death. He's spacey but he's not dumb.

I sat on the sofa and spread the pictures on the cushion next to me.

There was no clue to the photographer's identity. A bit of sleeve showed in the mirror in one picture, but in the others he or she was careful to keep out of the reflection's path.

Then, in the last picture, the one where the woman was putting on her sandals, I saw a backpack in the mirror hanging off the doorknob of the door, which seemed to have closed slightly since the earlier shots. It was book-size and urban-looking—like the packs some of my students used— with a reflective strip on the back. A key chain hung from the zipper tab. I couldn't make out anything about the keys, but the toy hanging from it was one of those little rubber horses with wires inside the legs so you could make it do things. A character from that claymation show that used to be on television when I was a kid, right before "Clutch Cargo."

Gumby, his name was.

No, that was the horse's friend. The green guy with the slanted head.

The horse was Pokey.

Pokey. It seemed like I'd been hearing a lot about him lately.

I stuffed the pictures back into the envelope, stuffed the envelope into my bag, and sat on the floor.

"Andrea," I said, half to myself and half out loud, "what is this all about?"

Lucas chomped on one of the towels that I'd used to sop up the water and tried to tempt me into a game of tug-of-war.

"Not right now, baby," I told him. "Right now I'm beginning to think our friend Altman is right. I ought to be talking to a lawyer. At Andrea's old firm. Find out what in the world she was up to."

Miss Osborne, the associate the Darling and Ueland receptionist passed my phone call to, wasn't enthusiastic.

"I'll level with you," she said. "We're a big firm and we cost a lot. I think with a matter as simple as an eviction you'd be better served by—"

"Look," I told her, "I can pay you cash today. I just need help right now. Give me one consultation and if it still doesn't seem like something you can do I'll go somewhere else."

"Really," she said, "I'm booked solid for the next three weeks. I just can't—"

I tried another tack.

"And I'd like to talk with you about something else," I said. "*Americans*, the magazine I work for, does a fair number of stories out of Massachusetts, and we like to have somebody in mind in case an issue comes up—copyright infringement maybe, or invasion of privacy. Can you suggest any local firms that might—"

"Well my gosh look at that," she said, "I *just* found out that one of my afternoon meetings has been canceled. It was at two o'clock."

"Okay," I said. "I'll be there."

9

I ALLOWED MYSELF PLENTY OF TIME—TOO MUCH TIME, AS IT TURNED out—to get lost in the thicket of one-way streets near South Station and ended up with forty minutes on my hands before my appointment at the firm. That's okay, I told myself as I parked, maybe I can walk the famous Freedom Trail (one of my first assignments for *Americans* had been taking pictures of tourists on the Freedom Trail during the Bicentennial), or maybe take a look at the harbor—whew!—maybe not!

Downtown the wind, which had been only a breeze in Cambridge, was fierce and concentrated. I could barely open the driver's side door and once I did I could barely stand upright. I stepped to the curb, held on tight to the parking meter, and fought off a newspaper that whipped itself around my ankles.

The natives huddled in doorways or sidled slowly down the sidewalk, their backs toward the storefronts.

"Wicked balmy out!"

An old woman with a metal cart full of grocery bags joined me in a drugstore doorway. She patted the load.

"This is what keeps me from flying away!" she said.

I inched down the sidewalk toward the sleek black and beige shaft my instructions told me was Franklin Place, shielding my eyes from the trash and dirt heaving around in the air, the song that plays in *The Wizard of Oz* when the witch flies by on her bicycle whining in my mind's ear. I finally backed into the building's revolving door and landed in its atrium: deluxe, warm, marble-lined, quiet except for the murmur of a fountain near an escalator to the mezzanine.

There was a coffee shop near the entrance. Fancy-shmancy with a black-and-white tile floor and a shiny Jules Verne-style espresso machine behind the counter. I sat down at a table about the size of a medium pizza and ordered a coffee. Then I walked to the window that separated the coffee shop from the rest of the lobby and inspected my reflection for wind shear.

The part in my hair had been driven from the right to the left side of my head. Could be worse, I thought.

I rearranged it with my fingers, unconsciously scanning the building directory, a back-lit board behind the security desk, at the same time.

"People could get killed out there," the waitress was saying. "They could go right through these plate glass windows. They—"

DARLING AND UELAND, the board said at the top.

HADLEY, EMERSON S.

HAGUE, H. PAUL

Then an empty space, then HATHAWAY, THOMAS.

I wondered how much longer it would take for someone to rearrange the letters to fill in the space where Andrea's name must have been. Everything else in the building seemed so slick, so ordered.

Two women entered the atrium from the revolving door, gasping from the wind, trying to juggle pocketbooks and huge briefcases. The woman nearest me was tiny, with black glossy hair in a precision haircut. She struggled, laughing, to untangle the huge silk scarf that she wore over the shoulders of her bright green wool coat. The other woman, in electric blue, was the same height as Andrea, and her hair was the same honey red.

Am I dreaming, I wondered. Could she—

The woman set her bag on the floor, took off her boots, and replaced them with a pair of black suede pumps that she pulled from a pocket in her coat. She glanced my way, checking her reflection in the other side of the glass, oblivious to me.

The woman gave her boots to the security guard, who bent to hide them under the desk. She patted him on the cheek, then walked with her pal to the elevators. Andrea wasn't the type to pat security guards on the cheek, I reminded myself. Or wear that much makeup. And besides, Andrea was dead.

Okay?

"You all right?"

The waitress had walked out from behind the counter.

"What?"

"You've been standing there staring an awful long time."

I guess I had.

I walked back to the table and sat down.

My coffee had gone tepid.

"You shouldn't leave your camera there like that," she said. "People steal stuff around here."

"Thanks."

She lowered her voice.

"I keep my wallet in the fridge."

"No kidding."

I tried to imagine Andrea in the coffee shop, wearing a

58

fancy wool coat like the women who'd just gone upstairs. What would she order—café au lait? Mochaccino with cinnamon? After all those years of austerity—fish stick suppers from the toaster oven for her and Patrick, day-old bread deals from the deli—I wondered if she'd ever adapted to yuppy ways.

A group of young women—girls, practically, painstakingly made-up, in heels and moussed hair—got off an elevator and came into the shop. One of them, with a heart-shaped face and enormous eyes, sat at the table next to mine while the others went to the counter to order. She was holding a magazine called *Today's Woman*. The woman on the cover had a *Wall Street Journal* in one hand and a baby bottle in the other.

"She just up and went to lunch and never came back," she yelled to them delightedly. "You should have seen Fred's face. He called her house and talked to her *mother*—"

The rest of the group collapsed with laughter.

"Her *mother*! Imagine Fred calling your *mother*!"

One hooted. She put her hands on her hips and screwed her face into a prissy look.

"Good afternoon, Mrs. Gillian. I'd like to remind Erin for me that sick days are a PRIVILEGE and not a RIGHT!"

The imitation must have been right on, because the rest of them howled and struggled to keep their drinks from spilling.

"How many does this make," asked one of them, "since Marsha—"

"Seven. No. Eight, if you count that I tried it for a day," another one said. "How did Marsha do it? Did they drug her? She knew how to work with Andrea, but Schuyler Kreps—"

They rolled their eyes heavenward simultaneously, as though they were responding to a cue from their director.

"He's getting weirder all the time," she continued. "I heard him shrieking at Erin yesterday morning because she put the staples in his contracts crosswise in the corner instead of up-

and-down. And she came in early for him! It's not her fault the stupid fish died. How was she supposed to . . . "

"—they didn't all die. Just a couple. His favorites, though."

"Poor Erin," one of them said.

A moment of silence.

"Poor Marsha," another added.

Poor fish, I thought.

I wondered what had happened to Marsha.

Big Eyes started up again.

"Fred had a conniption," she said, smiling. "The temp place said they couldn't send anybody until eleven tomorrow, so he's talking about using that new paralegal—"

"The guy?"

They collapsed into laughter again.

"The one who got his foot stuck in the shoe shine machine in the men's room? Good luck!"

More laughter.

"Fred would take anybody who walked in," Big Eyes said again. "Honest. He said so!"

A previously quiet one spoke up. "The agency can't help him out?"

More snorting and giggling.

I was feeling a little left out. When was the last time I sat around with a bunch of girlfriends and shot the breeze? You sure get to know a lot about a place over coffee or around the drinking fountain. A lot more than you'd learn from simply pretending to be a client.

I touched my hair to make sure the part was still there, then reached for my earlobes and was happy to find I was wearing my real-faux pearls. The ones I wear for dress-up occasions. Like asking Octavia for a raise.

I paid for my coffee, headed for the pay phones by the elevator bank, and canceled my appointment with Patricia Osborne.

60

"I'm figuring out how to take care of the problem myself," I told the secretary, happy not to have to lie.

Then I put on some Chapstick, smoothed my not particularly short dull brown miniskirt, and picked a little lint off my black stockings. *Really*, I thought. *Except for the boots*—I'd bought them on a shoot in Alaska seven years before, and I think they were intended for ice fishermen—*and the jacket*—which was raw on one cuff where Lucas had chewed on it in a fit of melancholy—*I almost look well-groomed.*

So I'm returning to work after fifteen years of child rearing, I told myself. *I'm Today's Woman. Fred will understand.*

10

THE DARLING AND UELAND LOBBY WAS A GRACEFUL BLEND OF VIC-torian oppression and Jetsonian futurism. A massive, coffin-like grandfather clock, back lit by fancy designer lighting, lurked in an alcove; a tastefully aged Oriental rug lay on top of the Stainmaster coffee-proof wall-to-wall carpet in the waiting area; *ComputerAge* magazine rubbed covers with *Forbes* on the low mahogany coffee table.

The receptionist, immaculately underwired, buffed, and coiffed—how did *she* deal with the wind tunnel outside? Did she get shot out of her car through a pneumatic tube?—skimmed her fingers across her telephone dashboard, barely looking at me.

"It's the twenty-two hundred," she said in my direction, "the collator. You know where to go."

I looked behind me to see who she was talking to.

Nobody.

Maybe I should have worn makeup—a wig, maybe—not the boots.

"I'm here," I told her, "for the temp job. To replace the secretary who just quit. I'm talking to Fred. My name is—"

The woman touched her fingers to her lips and giggled.

"Sorry. I thought you were the girl who fixed the copy machines. This is a madhouse today, you know?" She gestured toward one of the leather couches. "I'll tell him you're here, okay?"

I sat down and hid my feet under one of the tables. She murmured into her headset, then glided across the lobby with a bottle of Windex and a roll of paper towels in her hands.

She smiled at me. Maybe she was being extra solicitous because she was afraid she'd insulted me.

"Don't be nervous," she said. "Fred's a darling when he's not having a bad day. And besides, he's leaving tomorrow on vacation, so you won't have to see him for a while."

The door to the lobby was glass with a brass handle embedded in it. The woman spritzed the glass around the handle and polished it. I wondered if she did that after everybody came in or just for me.

"Take off your jacket," she said. "You can hang it in here—today, anyway. Tomorrow you can hang it in the closet behind your cubby. That's what the other girls do."

I hung it next to a flank of beige Burberry all-weather coats and glanced down at the closet floor. There was a nest of men's black rubber overshoes and one pair of women's pumps. They said NATURALIZER on the insides.

They looked a little dusty.

I glanced at my friend. She was crouching on the floor, busily picking at a piece of goo stuck to the threshold, her back to me.

I unlaced my boots, shoved them to the back of the closet, and stepped into the Naturalizers.

Cinderella! They were just my size.

I tried to figure out what to do with my camera. I was afraid somebody might swipe it from the closet.

I hung the strap diagonally cross my chest.

"Pretty handbag," the receptionist said. "Is it Italian?"

I was reading a *Forbes* article about declining panty hose sales when a paneled door to the inner offices slid open, and a tall, thin man wearing red suspenders and a floral bow tie, his white hair cut in a brush cut, motioned me to walk through.

"Quickly," he said. "Quickly. It stays open for eight seconds."

I stepped through and followed behind while he led the way to his office. Quickly, very quickly. With the upper part of his body leaning forward, as though that would help move things along.

"So Marge thought twice," he said. His voice was clipped and clear. "Well good. After all the business we've given that agency she should think twice."

He sat down at his desk, peered at me through his half-glasses, and plucked a piece of paper from a vertical file. His fingernails were manicured and glossy, with the cuticles squeezed back to show rising moons.

Uncertain my own hands could cut the mustard, I laced my fingers together with the nails on the inside, the way kids do when they start playing "Here is the church; here is the steeple," rested them on my knee, and tried to look modest, obliging, organized, and enthusiastic. The effort drew on a seldom-used part of my brain; I could feel the beginning of a headache.

"You're—"

"I'm—" I said—it came from nowhere—"Penny. Penny Kincaid."

Just half a lie. Maybe I'd only go to hell for half the usual sentence.

He started to write on the form but the pen dried out. He opened a drawer, pulled out a pencil, and pressed down so hard the lead broke off. He covered his face with his hands.

"The agency will send the information," he said.

I was trying not to stare at the Weight Watchers chart taped to the wall by his speakerphone. If I understood right, it showed that the man used to weigh nearly three hundred pounds.

"You're familiar with WordPerfect?" he asked. Then, before I could open my mouth, "Of course you are. All of Marge's are. How long will you be available?"

"I'm not sure."

"Are you looking for a permanent position?"

"Not right now."

He went quiet for a while.

"It's only fair to warn you," he said, "that the attorneys you will be working for are—"

He paused so long I got worried.

Psychopaths? About to be disbarred for felony convictions? Notorious sex perverts? I tried to maintain my demure yet level-headed manner.

"Demanding," he finally said.

"Okay."

"And remember," he said. "No chewing gum, no open-toed shoes, no Lycra, and no leather. No spraying hair, polishing nails, or keeping pets in your cubicle."

Whew. I tried to imagine the secretary who inspired the rules—a wild woman-child in a black spandex bodysuit, her hair whipped into a froth, a dog collar around her neck, her pet ferret tethered to her wrist with a leather strap . . .

"And it goes without saying," he continued, "that client confidentiality is of the utmost importance."

He paused for a moment, as if remembering an especially painful event.

"Especially in the elevators."

"Of course."

"Marie," he said, "will show you where you sit. She's my assistant. Marie will take care of support staff matters while I'm away."

Marie stood in the doorway, already summoned by the magic of Fred's machine. I followed her down a hallway lined on one side by secretarial cubicles, on the other by office doors.

At *Americans* the cubicles are designed so you can see the feet and at least part of the head of whoever is sitting in them—kind of like the stalls in the ladies' room. The assistants who sit in them can talk over the tops without standing up, pass things to one another, borrow dictionaries from one another's desks if they have to.

Here somebody could be lying dead in one and you'd never know. The partitions were five feet high and solid from bottom to top, upholstered in beige cloth. They reminded me of a book Claire gave me for my birthday once: *The Women in the Wall*, about an order of nuns who had themselves sealed up behind stone walls, with just a slit so somebody could shove food in. Marie led me into mine. The inside was stark: a computer keyboard, a CRT, a desktop laser printer, reference books, a phone, and cupboards along the top with fluorescent lights underneath.

Marie wiped some cookie crumbs off the desktop and into the trash can with the side of her hand.

"Honestly," she said. "Babies, these girls are. You practically have to wipe their bottoms."

She was sixtyish and formidable-looking. Mock turtleneck, sturdy blazer, wide ring-free hands.

"This one lasted ten days," she said. "I told Fred she'd never work out. Look at this!"

She pulled a forty-eight-pack of Dunkin' Donut Munchkins

out of my predecessor's bottom drawer and opened the lid. They were mostly powdered sugar, but a couple had red jam leaking out of them—my favorites.

"We already have mice," she said. "We'll have rats before you know it!"

She dumped the whole box in the trash basket. My heart sank with it.

"Disgusting," I said.

She looked at me approvingly.

"But you," she said, "I expect that you take your work seriously. Do you take shorthand?"

How old did she think I was? Was it the shoes?

"If you do," she said, "there's—"

A crashing sound erupted from behind a closed door across from my cubicle, followed by a muffled howl.

Marie remained calm.

"Schuyler Kreps," she said, barely raising her eyes. "Thar he blows."

The door flew open and an angry-looking guy, about my age, kind of blond, kind of beefy, with his sleeves rolled up and his necktie askew, tried to force a desk chair through his doorway by banging it first on one side of the door frame and then the other.

Marie still didn't look up.

He kicked the chair, then stood, panting, with his hands on his hips.

"He's been this way," she said quietly, "since he started losing his hair."

Then, in a louder, crisper voice, "May I help you, Schuyler?"

"You sure can, Marie." He was pouting now. "You sure can. You know this isn't the chair I wanted. You told me that the next time you ordered I could get a brown one. The back on this one doesn't even go up and down. Look at it!"

I wanted to tell him that if the back didn't adjust right it was because he had busted it, but I kept my mouth shut.

"You know what I think, Marie? I think this is Andrea's old chair and you're trying to get me to believe that it's new, aren't you? I don't want a used chair, Marie. I'm bringing this up at the partners' meeting."

He was pretending not to notice me.

"This is Penny, Schuyler. From the agency—"

"That's another thing, Marie. How come it took two hours to get somebody in here? You don't know how much ground I lost today already. I asked for an extension in *Gunter*. You know how that made me feel?"

"Schuyler, the temp is here now. Give her something to do. Now."

He glared at her, then at me.

"Forget it," he said. "I'm out of here."

He stormed down the hall.

I gave Marie a hand while she maneuvered the chair back into his office, which was big—twice as big as most of the others I'd seen as I'd walked down the hall—with a massive picture-window view of the Boston Common, the State House dome gleaming like the lid on a fancy casserole. A huge fish tank in a specially made wood cabinet sat in one corner; four photographs of Schuyler Kreps playing tennis hung on the wall above it.

Marie watched me look around the room.

"They made a big mistake," she said, "giving Schuyler this office. A big mistake."

I remembered the fish story I heard in the coffee shop.

"So Marie," I said, "who feeds those guys?"

"You do."

She looked at her watch.

"Don't worry about Schuyler," she said. "Not today, anyway. He's got a conference set up in the big room. You won't see him until tomorrow. All you need to do is make sure his time sheets are done. They're due in accounting by four."

"Okay."

She walked back down the hall.

I sat at my desk, switched on the disk drive, and felt a rush of smugness as the screen lit up. I knew something. I wouldn't have to fake everything.

It asked for my password.

Shit, I thought.

Drawers and cupboards were thumping in the cell next to mine. I found my way to the entrance and looked in.

It was one of the women I'd seen in the coffee shop. The one with the big eyes and heart-shaped face.

"Excuse me."

She didn't look up.

"Hi," I said. "How do I find out my password?"

She didn't say anything, just walked over to my desk and banged out some characters on my keyboard.

MVM.

I wrote it down on a Post-It and stuck it on my phone.

She looked at me with a glazed, impatient look, like a mother about to remind her three-year-old for the thousandth time to wash his hands after he uses the bathroom.

"What are you doing?" she said.

"Nothing, that is . . . "

She rolled her eyes.

"I mean," she said, "what do you want to get into?"

"Time sheets," I remembered. "I'm doing time sheets."

She reached into the plastic tray balanced on the ledge above my desk, plucked a piece of paper out, and started clicking away at the keyboard, fast—like a telegraph operator trying to get an emergency message out.

My hands started to sweat. Jesus—what was I doing in this place? I can type; I did most of my lecture notes on Claire's

69

Apple back home, but they were going to find me out in no time if I was supposed to move my hands that fast. Could they arrest me for this? For impersonating a secretary? And—oh god—what was it I'd said my name was?

The heart face was staring at me, alarmed.

"Are you okay? Are you sick or something? You want some Advil?"

I tried to relax.

She was rummaging through the desk's top drawer.

"There's gotta be some in here," she said. "Marsha used to take it all the time."

She looked at me again.

"I'm sorry," she said, "was I being mean to you? I'm sorry. Here—"

She found a bottle and shook two white capsules into my hand. Then she walked around to her desk and brought back an open can of Diet Coke.

"I guess we just stopped trying to get to know the girls who've been working for Schuyler. They hardly ever stay very long."

I washed the Advil down with the Coke.

"Here," she said, "I've got the program up for you."

She pulled a loose-leaf notebook from the shelf.

"The client numbers are in here," she said, pointing at another notebook.

"That's your chrono," pointing at another.

"And your office procedures."

She gave me another worried look.

"God," she said. "You do look awful."

Jesus, I thought. Maybe I should do something about my skin. Hydrate. Exfoliate. Peel, maybe. Whatever it is Octavia's always having done.

"Take a break," she said. "I'll get these started."

She typed away, looking occasionally into the notebook, then turned back to me.

"Here you go," she said. "I did two days for you."

She flipped her index finger through the stack of sheets.

"Looks like you'll be doing overtime tonight," she said. "Your pay gets docked if you don't get them done on time. Call Marie and tell her you'll need dinner."

I started to think about Lucas. I usually walked him at five, after I got home from the office.

"Don't look so worried," she said. "Plenty of people work late here. Marie will get one of the mail room guys to wait downstairs for the cab with you if it gives you the creeps. And the security guards make rounds after seven."

After seven? What would Lucas do?

"Why?" I asked. I remembered what the coffee shop waitress had said about keeping her wallet in the refrigerator. "Do you have break-ins here?"

She lowered her voice.

"Not in ages," she said. "But people get nervous around here anymore. Especially since . . . "

She bit her lip to keep herself from continuing.

"Since the lawyer got killed? Andrea Hale?"

She nodded. "You know about her?" she asked. "She worked"—she jerked her chin toward the office next to Schuyler Kreps's, the one with the closed door —"in there."

She had an exaggerated spooked-out look on her face.

"I mean," she said, "she wasn't killed in there, but that's where she worked and it gave everybody the creeps."

She pulled her sweater around her shoulders to ward off the chill she was giving herself.

"I mean," she said. "There she was, working in the morning, and then there she was, dead."

I was getting chilly, too.

71

"I'm pretty sure," she said, "it's why Marsha, the secretary who used to work for Schuyler and her"—she avoided saying Andrea's name—"left. It just cracked her up. She's not even doing temp work." She stared at the closed office door.

"I don't see how Darthea does it."

"Who's Darthea?"

She gave me her long-suffering look again.

"The other lawyer you work for," she said. "I don't see how she goes in there every day. Sits at Andrea Hale's desk. I won't go in there for anything."

She looked darkly at Andrea's old door, then back at me.

"I'm Lorna," she said softly. "Call me if you need anything."

She went back to her cubicle.

I turned to the keyboard, touched the Return key, slowly got the hang of it: client name, code, a description of what Kreps had done on the case, the amount of time, in sixths of an hour. It would have moved along okay if Kreps's handwriting were a little bit clearer. I was having a hell of a time translating the client names so I could look up the numbers. What I thought was a woman's name—Cass Karismo—turned out to be "Karisma Cars"; Mister Softweave turned out to be "Master Software, Inc."; "Cousin Citgo" turned out to be "Concerned Citizens Assn." etc.—slow going to say the least.

Something thwacked out of the air onto the right-hand side of my desk. A brick, maybe. No, a Filofax. A strained-looking woman's face appeared at the cubicle door.

"Where's Erin?"

"She's not here. I'm the temp."

"Another temp? I can't stand this. It's—" She stopped herself. "Sorry. It's not your fault."

She was the blond I'd seen in the lobby. The one who'd given the guard her boots. Now I couldn't figure out how I'd thought she was Andrea for even a minute. She was at least ten years younger and twenty times more hyper.

"Don't worry about the Filofax now," she said. "I've got to get a draft settlement agreement over to Adler and Reitz in half an hour before they back out."

She threw her coat over the top of the partition.

"Here," she said. "Do it straight into the machine while I say it."

Darthea, I guessed. She was wearing Norell, the same perfume Octavia wore. It was giving me bad-boss flashbacks.

I hit the New Document key and typed while she talked. Not so bad—a lot easier than following something printed with your eyes while you type—except for the little sucking sound the woman made every time I made a mistake.

Eight pages later she hit the Print button herself, stood by the printer while the pages dropped out, and disappeared with them.

Five-fifteen. Damn. I pulled up the time sheet program again. Dock my pay? Doesn't anybody around here belong to a union? Maybe I ought to start organizing.

The phone buzzed. I picked it up.

"This is Schuyler Kreps," the voice said, big, puffed up, all arrogance. "I need a Band-Aid. Now. In the Ueland Room." Then he hung up.

You do, do you?

I unsnapped the side pocket of my camera case, where I keep my lifesaving supplies—baby pocket knife, spare key to the loft, twenty-dollar bill for placating muggers, Band-Aid—and headed for the lobby.

The receptionist pointed toward the door of a huge glass-walled room. The drapes were drawn.

"Wait a minute," she said. "Don't go in yet." She pulled a compact out of her drawer and checked her face. "Okay," she said, straightening her back and smiling. "Go ahead, open it."

I opened the door to the conference room. A big tanned man with a toupee, his shirt unbuttoned three buttons, a gold

73

cross on a chain around his neck, sat at the center of the table. His eyes were closed.

Schuyler Kreps sat at one end, his hand still on the phone.

I held the Band-Aid toward him.

"No," he said, "It's Gus. Mr. Huntoon. He's got a paper cut."

The tan man held his right hand, big as an oven mitt, toward me, the fingers spread. An inch-long thread of red gleamed in the webbing of flesh between his thumb and index finger.

His eyes flicked open.

"What's your name?" he said.

His breath smelled like Tic Tacs.

"Penny."

"Penny," he said, shutting his eyes again. "Would you do me a favor?"

I wasn't sure.

"Would you put it on for me?"

His skin looked funny. Then I realized that it was because his lips had faded to a color lighter than the rest of his face.

I glanced at Kreps. He jerked his head up and down, begging me with his eyes to do as I was asked.

The big guy looked like he was going to keel over.

"Maybe," I said, "you ought to put your head between your knees."

The man exhaled—a compressed hiss like the sound a truck makes when the brakes go on—and lay his head on the table.

I opened the Band-Aid wrapper, peeled the protective paper from the adhesive, and spread the Band-Aid over the cut.

"I don't know," I said. "That's kind of a weird place for a Band-Aid. I don't know if it will stay on when you move your fingers around."

74

His eyes were still shut. Kreps motioned me toward him and handed me a piece of paper. It had a smear of blood in one corner.

"Do me another favor," he said. "Could you type this over?"

"Sure," I said, and walked back out into the lobby.

"Did he talk to you?"

It was the receptionist.

"Who?"

"Mr. Huntoon."

"Yeah," I said, remembering the moan. "Well, sort of."

She spied the piece of paper in my hand.

"Are you going back in?"

"I guess so," I said, "when I finish this."

She smiled. "I'll do it for you and save you the trouble. Just leave it here when you're done."

She tucked a stray wisp of hair back into her hairdo, then reached inside her blouse and straightened her shoulder pads.

"He has a helicopter," she said. "It lands on his office building."

"No kidding."

"He used to be a boxer. And he still looks good. And honey, he's loaded. He's got the biggest construction company in—" The phone flickered. "Darling and Ueland," she said. "May I help you?"

The piece of paper was the first page of a table of contents for a prospectus. No way, I thought, I'd be able to do all these indented columns right. I pulled the document index up on the computer screen and scanned through for the original. Twelve pages, fifteen pages—I had no idea what the document was named.

I could, I thought, use Wite-Out on the blood. I was very familiar with Wite-Out. My college papers had been covered with it.

I rummaged through the drawers. More Tums. No Wite-Out.

I went next door.

"Lorna," I whispered, "can you help me?"

She came to my desk, leaned over my shoulder, and tapped into a subindex, then a sub-subindex.

"God," she said. "Fred would have a heart attack if he knew Marsha kept these old documents in here. We're supposed to clean up—"

She was in a special Huntoon directory.

"—every three months."

The table of contents flashed on the screen. I hit Print and waited for the finished product.

I brought the sheet to the lady at the front desk and got back to the time sheets. Other secretaries were leaving for the day; over the partitions I could see the tops of closet doors opening and closing, and I could hear the muffled sounds of boots on carpet and voices calling good-bye.

My stomach whined like a laser printer heating up; I felt a little woozy from having missed lunch. I mustered just enough self-control to keep from plowing through the trash for the baby donuts. I started a systematic inspection of my desk drawers. *Where there's Donut Munchkins*, I told myself, *there's got to be something else good; peanut butter crackers? Little Debbie Snack Cakes?*

More Advil, tidy rubber-band-bound stacks of Darthea Cox's and Schuyler Kreps's business cards, a paper clip chain, a box of HiPROMIN flake food for tropical fish that didn't even tempt me, envelopes, Kleenex travel packs, message pads, Post-Its . . .

The bottom drawer in the file cabinet was my last hope. I yanked it, but it wouldn't open more than five or six inches, so I yanked again.

Lorna leaned out of her cubicle.

"Don't bother," she said. "That drawer's been busted for months. There's extra file space in the file room if you want it."

"Okay, Lorna. Thanks."

Something was wedged between the metal frame that supported the file folders and the inside top of the drawer. I reached in with both hands and tugged on what felt like crumpled cardboard. It resisted, then gave way. I pulled out the offending hunk, and the drawer slid free. It was empty all the way to the back; no food, no more Advil, even.

The hunk was a manila folder, and the cover had said TO DO on it in black marker before I ripped it in half.

"Amazing," Lorna said from the other side of the wall. "Don't let too many people around here know you can fix things like that or they'll be making you assemble bookcases."

"Thanks for the tip."

The folder was full of half-completed expense reports, time sheets, subscription renewal forms for legal publications—all for Andrea. Or Andrea S. Hale, Esquire, or ASH, or, in the case of the subscription renewals, Attorney Andrew Hale. Anything that had a date on it was from the six-month period before Andrea was killed. There were lists of things to do, written in handwriting that wasn't Andrea's, and lists of things to do written in handwriting that was Andrea's. "Marsha: Call Ellen Grant re Tuesday depo; reschedule meeting re evidence committee; find room for WBA lunch; call McHugh's clerk re new date for *Bruce* summary judgment; order covers for *Meath* record appendix." And single notes, too, dashed on memo paper with Andrea's name printed at the top: "Marsha: *Please* order the *Roos* files from dead storage ASAP," and "Marsha: *Please* go to Marie's office yourself and ask for my change of beneficiary card. I need ASAP." This last without a date.

Fascinating.

I pulled the poem I'd found in Andrea's sweatshirt from my wallet and compared the handwriting to the handwriting on the notes. No doubt about it; it was the same script. A little more hurried, a little more urgent on the office notes, maybe, but look—there were the same blunt-tailed *g*'s, the same wide-looped *l*'s and *b*'s, the same—

"Oh my god, I can't believe it."

Lorna was at my shoulder. I folded the poem in half and placed it under the pile I was keeping.

"If I were you," she went on, "I'd jam that junk back into that file cabinet and pretend you never saw it."

She looked at me darkly.

"Or *you'll* be the one who has to go through it all and figure out what she didn't do."

She sighed.

"I wondered for a while there if Marsha was doing something like this. Sometimes she'd just sit there with the desktop all cleared off and I knew she couldn't have gotten everything done. So that's what she did with everything. Stuffed it in a drawer. Honest. Do yourself a favor. Put it back."

She went back to her cubby, then hissed at me from the entrance: "Or get rid of it."

I took out the time sheets, the expense reports, and the note about changing the beneficiary, and put them in my bag. Then I stuffed the folder back in the drawer.

Lorna, now in her coat and hat, came around again.

"Don't forget to sign off when you leave," she said. "Fred gets real upset about that."

What doesn't Fred get upset about?

I tried to speed things up.

Poor Lucas. If I hit a snag in New York I could call my downstairs neighbor and ask him to take Lucas around the block.

I could call Jack, but by the time Jack got in from Lincoln I'd be on my way home. Besides, I had Jack's key.

Six-fifteen. Darthea ran out, leaving me a number where I could call her. Kreps left, too, without saying a word.

Six forty-five. Now that I could decipher all the client names my fingers were flying.

I transmitted the documents to the printer and got up to stretch.

"Printer Busy," the screen told me. "You are document no. 17."

Great, I thought. I'll be lucky if I'm out of here in an hour. Another wave of panic for Lucas rose in my stomach.

I straightened up my desk, which took all of four seconds.

A guy was droning into a Dictaphone machine in an office around the corner. *Dear uppercase C-chuck colon I regret to inform you that* . . .

I looked down the hallway. Most of the secretarial stations were empty, but a couple of what looked like night-shift typists—one was a guy with a beard and jeans—were settling in.

Remembering the coffee lady's warning about thieves, I took my camera out of my drawer, then walked into Darthea's office.

My conversation with Lorna had prepared me to meet Andrea's ghost, but the room was the most unlike-Andrea place possible. I couldn't imagine her in it.

Fifteen or twenty rust-color accordion-pleated file folders, all threatening to burst at the seams, formed a ring around Darthea's desk chair. Yellow Post-It messages shingled the base and stem of her desk lamp, most of them with the letters ASAP written somewhere on them. Three partly filled cups of black coffee rode in the sea of papers and open books on her desk; a vase of dead lilies had dropped pollen on an open yellow pad next to the phone.

Two framed posters hung crookedly on the wall—one advertised the Boston Flower Show, the other was a view of sailboats on the Charles taken with Vaseline on the camera lens to make everything look misty and romantic.

I turned off the light, opened the blinds, and stared at the evening view of the city—the snake of red brake lights sneaking around the Common; the filigree of tree branches and holiday lights against the brownstones on Boylston Street; the old-fashioned gas lamps leading up the State House steps.

Lamps like that wouldn't last a half hour in New York before somebody threw a bottle at them, I thought. Why doesn't that happen here?

I could imagine Andrea standing at the same window, thinking. She loved vistas, big views, panoramas.

Once, just after we'd first met, she talked me into hiking in the Adirondacks. We drove overnight from Rochester, then started up Mount Marcy in the morning twilight. I was wearing sneakers, not hiking boots; my feet were killing me and I kept stopping to rest. Andrea couldn't wait to get to the top. She moved fast, growing happier and more energetic the higher we climbed.

When we reached the peak the sky was opaque with clouds. We were about to turn back when they lifted—suddenly, absolutely, like a bedspread taken from a clothesline—and there was this monumental, heart-stopping view of the rest of the range, the valleys, the notches, the ocean of trees, 360 degrees around us. Andrea sat on a rock and sobbed at the sight.

It was the only time I ever saw her cry; even when the cops came to school and told her that her parents had died she did her crying locked in the bathroom.

I leaned against the bookcase and framed a photograph of the view in my mind's eye. Not the kind of thing I take, usually. Too romantic. Too derivative. But still . . . I opened my camera case.

The overhead light flashed on and I spun toward the door.

"¡Dios mio!"

A small dark-skinned woman, a yellow plastic bag draped over one arm, stood frozen in the doorway.

"Excuse me," I said. "I mean *perdóname*."

The woman stepped into the office. One of her eyes turned out a little, so it was hard to tell exactly what she was focusing on, but she seemed to be studying me.

She pulled a trash can from under the desk, dragged it across the floor, and emptied it into a canvas Dumpster on wheels that stood in the hall outside the door. Then she shook the plastic bag open and lined the trash can with it. Her movements were tight, efficient, pissed off.

I scavenged my brain for Spanish words, trying to put together "I didn't mean to scare you."

"*Perdóname*," I said again. "*No quería a—*" She dusted the chair arms with a feather duster.

"I speak English," she said. Then, very clearly and slowly, "very well."

I couldn't tell how old she was. Maybe twenty-five, maybe forty. There was something young-looking about the way she carried her head, and a girlishness about her features: she had a wide mouth, full, fleshy cheekbones; and her thick blue-black ponytail was secured by a rubber band with translucent green balls attached to it. But she didn't wear makeup, didn't smile, had none of the bounce of the secretaries in the coffee shop.

She wore a cotton smock with snaps down the front—the same smock you see on the guy who checks your oil, on the checkout clerks in the grocery store, and on the mammogram technicians at the breast clinic, except this one was light yellow and had a patch sewn on the front pocket that said

WHITEGATE CLEANING SERVICES. It was meant to be an overshirt to protect the clothes underneath it, but this woman was so small, and the garment so big, that it fit like a dress.

She straightened the heap of books in the chair, dusted the phone, and untangled the cord that controlled the window blinds. Then she scanned the disarray on the desk with a disgusted look and dumped the dead flowers into the Dumpster.

"You know her?" she said to me. "This"— she fanned her arm in the air above the desk—"this dirty attorney?"

"No," I said. "Not really. I only just started here today. I'm a secretary. I was taking a break."

She went on with her work, picking scraps of paper off the floor, adjusting the books in the bookcase so the spines were flush with the edges of the shelves, dusting around me, ignoring me, as though she'd made me disappear through mind control.

She walked back to the hall and returned with a paper cone of flowers in her hand. Daisies, it looked like, with ferns for filler.

She knocked the pollen from the legal pad into the trash, gathered and capped the scattered pens, and made a tidy stack of the books. Then she peeled the paper from the daisies and lowered the stems into the vase on the desk slowly and tenderly, like somebody dipping a newborn into its bath.

She closed her eyes again, then opened them and looked toward me.

"Desecration," she said. "This woman desecrates the memory of my friend."

"The flowers are for Andrea Hale?"

She looked at me hard. This time both eyes seemed to work together.

"Yes," she said.

She tensed, backing off from me a little.

"You knew her?" she asked. "But you said this was your first day to work. Today. How could you know her?"

She looked around the room like she was trying to figure out if I'd stolen anything.

Her eyes landed back on me.

"What were you doing here," she said, "in the darkness?"

She pointed at the camera in my hand.

"In the darkness," she said again, "with that?"

Wait a minute, I thought, reeling a little from the blitz. She ought to be the one practicing law, not these bozos with the Dictaphones.

Her hand moved to the phone. That's all I need, I thought. She's going to call security. They'll call the temp agency and find me out in five minutes. This is big time, I thought. My students—I thought. Lucas—

"Wait a minute," I said.

I opened the pocket on my camera case, got my wallet, fumbled through the credit card slots, and came up with a postage-stamp-size picture of Andrea and me taken in a dime-store photo booth the winter before she left RIT. I was mugging in the shot, and the top of my head was absorbed into the top margin of the print, making me look like I had a flat-top. Andrea, her hand cupping my chin as though she were trying to pull me back into the frame, looked serene and happy. Her hair hung in a heavy braid over one shoulder and she looked straight into the camera's eye.

I held the picture out to the woman.

"Here," I said. "She was my friend, too. Andrea."

She took it from me, zigzagging her gaze from it to me three or four times to confirm that the one girl's features matched my own.

She handed it back to me.

"When was it?" she said. "When was the picture? You were teenagers? From the same neighborhood?"

"Teenagers," I said. "That's right."

I'd been nineteen, twenty maybe; Andrea had been a little younger. We'd been shopping for Christmas presents. Something for her brother. A model to build. A submarine, maybe. Something military. I remember giving her grief about it. I hadn't thought about that trip since it happened, hadn't looked at the picture for years.

The woman sat down in one of the chairs opposite the desk, pulled a pack of cigarettes out of her smock pocket, and offered one to me.

"No thanks," I said. "I don't want one."

Although I did, of course, but I'd promised myself a new light meter if I could keep off them another six months.

She lit up, then gestured toward the hall.

"They think they forget her," she said. "They put this"— she lowered her gaze toward the file folders spilling their guts on the floor—"slob in here and think no one remembers, but I—"

She waved her hand through the smoke toward me, then pointed to the empty desk chair.

"She used to smoke with me here. At night. She would ask me to stay. Close the door. Tell me to put my feet up."

She got up, closed the door, then returned to the chair. She didn't put her feet up; she stretched them in front of her, crossing her legs at the ankles.

"She was always working so hard," she said. "I told her she shouldn't do so much. How would she get a husband, staying alone here every night, every weekend, nobody to talk to but the cleaner?"

Funny, I thought, she never picked up that Andrea was married. Didn't she wear a ring?

But Andrea would have seemed like a single person given the hours she kept.

She flicked the ash from her cigarette into one of the coffee cups.

"'But look at you, Teresa,' she would say to me. 'Look at how hard you work. We're the same kind of people, Teresa.'"

The woman seemed unaware of what an amazing mimic she was; she had captured Andrea's phrasing, the soft crispness of her voice, so perfectly that I caught my breath. She knew Andrea better than most people, I suspected; she'd probably seen more of her than Jack had the past few years.

But since when did Andrea smoke cigarettes? She never did at school. And the condo didn't smell like cigarettes.

And when did she start writing bad love poems on corny stationery?

There were footsteps in the hall. They came near. I froze, but Teresa was relaxed. Then whoever it was went away.

"Don't worry," she said. "They're gone now."

Now that she wasn't so wary of me her face had softened. She eased her heels out of her shoes and sighed.

A perfect corkscrew of smoke floated from the end of her cigarette and dissolved against the ceiling.

"Her clothes," she said, watching me watch the smoke, "they were beautiful. All the seams sewn down, the buttons covered with cloth, everything lined, everything beautiful. Wool gabardine," she said. "Cashmere. Viyella."

"Viyella," she repeated. "Do you have clothes made from viyella?"

I doubted it.

"No," I said.

She looked satisfied. Of course I didn't have clothes made out of viyella. I wasn't Andrea.

"It's very soft," she said. "Very expensive."

She held the cigarette pack toward me again.

"You sure?" she said.

I wanted her to keep talking, to stay with me, tell me everything she knew about Andrea.

"Okay," I said.

Maybe I didn't need the new light meter so much after all.

Teresa lit my cigarette with hers.

"She ever give you her clothes?" she asked.

"No."

When I first knew Andrea she hardly had any clothes. Jeans, overalls, flannel shirts, floppy hats. If they were good enough for Janis Joplin, we figured, they were good enough for us. None of this wool gabardine, cashmere, viyella stuff.

"She did to me," she said. "A whole box once. Everything almost new. I sent the coat to my mother, but I kept the skirts and blouses. She was a saint. It's not true what the papers say about her. She helped my cousin when he got in trouble. For nothing. She went with him to the court." Her voice grew softer and softer as she talked.

Now she pulled a wallet out of her pocket.

"Here," she said. "Here. I have a picture, too."

She handed me a small color photograph of a little girl, two or three years old, with fat cheeks, brown hair, and huge brown eyes. She was sitting in someone's lap—there was an adult arm around her waist—but you couldn't tell who it was.

"My daughter," she said. "She's in Guatemala with my mother. I live here for work. For money. I send it to them. I baby-sit, too," she said. "For a family in Charlestown. That's where I live. In their house. The Burleys. They gave me my own TV to learn English."

She looked at the picture again, then put it back in her wallet.

"*Triste*," she said, pointing to her eyes.

They were full of tears.

"The picture," she said. "It makes me very sad."

My eyes were stinging, too.

"*Triste*," I said. "I feel bad for you."

She pulled a paper towel from her roll, tore it in half, gave me a piece, and scrubbed her cheeks with the other one.

"She gave me money once," she said. "When the baby was sick. For better medicine. The nuns said she would die if she didn't get it. Andrea gave me the money. She would always help me. She said she would try to figure out a way—"

She was really crying now.

To what? Get the baby here? Get the woman a job with more money? Take care of her immigration papers?

"I wanted to pay her back the money," she said. "She told me not to, but I wanted to and then—"

"Andrea died," I said.

"He killed her," she said at the same time.

She was sobbing, her head collapsed forward on her chest, her entire body shuddering and shaking.

I sat in the chair next to hers, tried to take her hand, but she pulled it away.

"She wouldn't have wanted the money," I said. "All Andrea ever wanted to do was help people. She was like that."

She sat still, trying to calm down, hiccupping. "I wanted to pay her back," she said. "I made her flan once. I loaned her my car—not my car—the car Mr. and Mrs. Burley let me use to drive the children—when hers broke once, but I wanted to do more. I wanted to pay her back—"

"So you bring flowers."

She nodded.

I wondered how much they cost her. Three-fifty a bunch, I figured. Maybe more. A lot of money on cleaner's pay.

We sat there in silence. Then Teresa walked toward the window, studied what she could see of her reflection, and toyed with the elastic band around her ponytail.

"Teresa," I said, "is there something about Andrea that you want to tell me? Was there something she said to you—?"

She walked to the door.

I took one of the Post-Its from Darthea's desk and wrote my name and number on it.

"Lib-by," she started to read.

I put my finger to my lips.

"Yes, Libby," I said. "But around here they call me Penny."

"Libby," she said. Then, "Just one question."

"What is it?"

"What was Andrea's brother's name?"

"Patrick," I said.

"How much cream did she like in her coffee?"

"None," I said. "She liked it black." Or she did anyway, back in Rochester.

"Okay."

I must have passed some kind of test.

She looked up and down the hall, making sure no one was near.

"Will you be here," she said, "in this same place Monday?"

"Yes," I said.

I could be if I had to.

"I want to give you something," she said. "Something for Andrea."

"Okay," I said. "That's fine."

She stuffed the roll of paper towels back into its pocket on the rolling Dumpster, then looked in at me one last time.

"Too bad," she said, "you didn't work here before. You could have smoked with us."

11

"LUKEY BOY," I SAID, SLICING TAKEOUT CHICKEN OFF THE BONE FOR him, "this won't be forever. A couple of days, that's all." I didn't teach Monday; maybe I could move Tuesday's class to the evening. "Then it will be you and me again in the afternoon, strolling around Fresh Pond, scaring squirrels. Soon. Honest. You'll see."

It was Saturday morning. I'd hired a lady to walk Lucas in the afternoons while I was downtown. "Tia," her name was. She advertised at the Huron Avenue bus stop, right between the notices for "Eclectic Witch Seeks Roommate with Similar Interests" and "Clay Therapy."

"It'll be fun. Honest. You'll learn how to get along with other people besides me."

Lucas wasn't buying it, I was sure, but he made fast work of the chicken, then begged for more.

"I talked to her for a long time on the phone. She sounds real nice. She has two dogs of her own. And she doesn't smoke, she says."

Which is more than I can say for myself, I thought, wincing at the memory of my lapse in Andrea's office. I could still taste the nicotine on my gums.

"Just for a little while. Honest."

But would she remember to come? Would she remember to look through his fur for burrs and ticks when they got back home? Talk with him a little bit the way he likes? Let him off the leash when they're in front of the house so he can run up the steps by himself? Somehow I didn't think so.

I'd had a fat night's sleep but still hadn't recovered from my seven hours at Darling and Ueland. Clerical speed and accuracy are taxing, especially when you're like me and used to working with a machine that only has one button on it.

It was a blank Saturday, like the ones you used to have when you were a kid: no phone calls, no car repairs to get done, no taxes to prepare. The refrigerator had enough food in it; my laundry was clean. I should have felt relaxed, but I didn't. I kept thinking about Teresa, watching other people's kids so she could afford to support her own a continent away. And Andrea. And Teresa and Andrea together, forging a friendship at night in a near-empty skyscraper while the rest of the world washed dinner dishes or watched TV.

The weather report said chance of snow; the fragment of sky I could see through the living room window looked tarnished and cold. When I went out to buy the papers the air had that metallic tang that means something's on its way.

I paid some parking tickets, rinsed out my tights, and fooled with the thermostat. I stood at the kitchen counter and read the whole *New York Times*, including the business section, and the whole *Boston Globe*, including the classifieds and my new favorite column, "Confidential Chat," where regular people correspond anonymously with one another, looking for advice or wanting to know if anybody knows some old household hint or recipe.

"Dear Chatters," somebody wrote today. "Does any reader remember that old recipe for chocolate cake that uses a jar of Hellman's mayonnaise?" and "Does anyone remember how to make a small ornamental Christmas tree using- discarded *Reader's Digest*s?"0

There was an ad for an auction of antique photographs in Lexington. Maybe I could pick something up for Dan, I thought, then marveled at myself for forgetting that Dan Sikora and I had been over with as a couple for more than six months.

I called Claire, which is what I always do when I have that old feeling I can't really put my finger on.

The baby could open its eyes now, she said. The chart in the book said so. She'd been holding a flashlight against her stomach to give it something to look at.

"What are you trying to do?" I asked her. "Make the kid go blind? She can't exactly run out to the store and pick up some Ray Bans, you know."

"Oh, honestly, Libby," she said. "You just don't know what it's like. You want them to be happy and—you know—*stimulated*—even when they're still inside you. *Especially* when they're still inside you. And what makes you so sure the baby's a she?"

Did I detect a new note of madonnalike superiority in Claire's voice? We'd been best friends for fourteen years and all, but suddenly I wasn't sure my loyalty could last through prebirth education attempts and then the baby French class, baby yoga, and whatever the heck else all my formerly normal New York friends were now subjecting their offspring to.

Could this really be the same old Claire—the woman who used to gag when she saw a Huggies commercial on TV?

"Of course it's a girl," I told her. "You're a girl aren't you? You went to a women's college didn't you? You're not buying one of those giant strollers with a ski rack, are you? They don't fit down the aisle at the deli. I saw a lady get stuck there with one once. They had to get the Jaws of Life from the fire department to free the baby. They—"

"Oh God, Libby," she said. "Honestly."

Then, in her old, chipper Claire voice. "Bye, Lib. Love you. Gotta go."

I hung up, mad at myself for having deprived myself of an hour of heart-to-heart by being a smartass. I'd wanted to talk with Claire about Andrea, about Jack, about Dan. Too bad.

What did Andrea do when she'd felt like this? Wrote another brief, most likely. Tossed off a law journal article.

And Teresa? She probably didn't have time to feel like this. She was probably giving four kids their baths.

Lucas pressed his head against my legs. He was getting a little gray under the chin, and napping more than he used to. I rubbed the stubble on his muzzle.

"So buddy," I said. "What if it turns out to be a boy after all? How's anybody going to know what to do with him? Are we gonna throw Frisbees with him in Washington Square Park? Teach him how to catch with his mouth?"

Not that I really thought for a minute that Claire would end up staying in New York with the baby. No, she'd sell the loft—if she hadn't already—move to a nice little stone house somewhere on the Hudson, and write articles for *Horticulture* magazine about growing delphiniums, which she'd been threatening to for the last ten years, and I'd never see her or little whazzit ever again.

Our next-door neighbor was doing his laundry. Columns of warm air rose from the vent in his first-floor window, twisted around themselves, and dissolved into the sky. Suddenly the air seemed thick and heavy; then I realized that the thickness was snowflakes, big ones, drifting every which way through the air, as though they hadn't caught the hang of coming down yet, then after a few minutes organizing themselves into something more serious, more ordered—a real fall, the flakes coming faster, and faster.

A bizarre fantasy flew into my mind, imposed itself on the backdrop of snow without asking my permission: for a moment I saw Dan, me, Lucas, and a baby together in a yard—tiny, like a scene in a shaken-up snow globe. The baby dropped a mitten, red, like its snowsuit, on the ground; Dan and I both reached to pick it up.

Just as suddenly the figures disappeared and the scene was like it really was: the darkening sky, the steam, the gray shingled wall, the bare black tree branches with the deltas of snow collecting in their crotches. No Dan. No snowsuit. No mitten.

Jesus, I thought, spinning away from the window. Where did that come from?

It was four o'clock. I made a peanut butter sandwich, got into my pajamas, and spent the evening in bed, reading *The Clan of the Cave Bear*—the only romance novel I've ever really liked, most likely because it's set six million years before women shaved their legs. Lucas lay on my feet, sleeping and chasing imaginary squirrels. I dropped the book and burrowed deeper under the blankets.

For the first time in weeks I let myself wonder where Dan was, let myself remember what it was like to lay my head in his armpit while we slept.

"Me lonely," I grunted to Lucas as I turned out the light. "Me want man."

I imagined Jack asleep on his army cot within spitting distance of his mother, dreaming about exploded-view patent applications for his cameras. I imagined Sammy on the other side of the room, sweating in his sleep, trying to figure out how he'd make his next child support payment without selling the car.

Maybe not, I thought, and conked out.

12

MY ACUTELY TUNED MANHATTAN INTRUDER-SENSORS YANKED ME awake—heart slamming, muscles tight, pupils fully dilated. I rose to my elbows and scanned the room, human radar, ready to distinguish the shadows that were furniture from the shadows that were a guy in a ski mask with a stiletto in his hand.

Lucas yawned; I shoved him in the side to keep him awake.

"Listen!" I hissed.

To what? Now everything was quiet. I strained to hear the nearly invisible slide of a window, the feeble creak of a door, the clink of a metal chain disengaging from its lock. Maybe I dreamed whatever wakened me.

But there it was again. A scraping sound, like a metal stool being dragged across a concrete floor. Except there wasn't a metal stool or chair anywhere in the condo; the bedroom I was in was the only furnished room, if you call a mattress, a crate, and a drafting table—courtesy of Argus—furnished. The sound—fragment of a sound was more like it—evaporated every time I thought I'd located it. The bathroom? No. The other bedroom? It had wall-to-wall carpet—nothing could make a sound like that in there. The stairwell to the basement? Was it a ladder?

I closed my eyes, trying to heighten my senses. Instead a double-page *Time* magazine spread, circa 1964, opened across my inner field of vision: pen-and-ink portraits of the Boston Strangler's victims—nurses, bookkeepers, widows, teachers. Everybody nice—like you and me. Then the block of text next to each face explaining the lady's condition when found, strangled with her own stockings, arranged by the killer in his lunatic signature bow.

You didn't hear too much about that guy anymore. Was he alive? Was he still locked up? *Americans* hadn't done one of those "Where Are They Now?" articles about him.

Pipe down, I chided myself. That was back in the days of real nylons. They probably reminded the guy of his mother—how he used to rub his cheek against her calves or something. You can bet, I reassured myself, she didn't wear cotton/Lycra tights—the only leg wear I had hanging around.

There it was again. A little louder. Just outside the high bank of bedroom windows.

Maybe it's Jack, I thought, making sure the gutters are cleared out. Otherwise they clog up with ice and the water wrecks your ceilings. I read about that somewhere. Or it's somebody shoveling the walk. Except the sound wasn't the strong rhythmic sound of a shovel; it was tentative, furtive. And who cleans gutters and shovels sidewalks in the middle of the night?

The scrape came again, this time followed by a muffled clang that sent Lucas staggering to his feet.

"Atta boy," I said softly, more for my benefit than his, trying to soothe myself. "You can keep that up."

Why the hell hadn't I gotten a phone installed in the bedroom? The jack was there; it would have been cheap. I could call from the kitchen, but what if somebody was in the living room? And why had the architect who designed this place put the windows so high? Sure, the view of the warehouse in the lot behind wasn't so pretty, but—

I pushed the crate I used for a night table across the room and stood on it.

Even on tiptoe I couldn't see out. I put my biography of Marion Post Wolcott on top of the crate and tried again, thinking that if I could wrap my fingers around the sill I could hoist myself up.

The book started to slip but I was almost there.

I'll scare the guy, I thought. He'll just—

Light blasted my face. Harsh, bright, laser-style. I spun away, fell off the crate, and slammed back-first against the floor, just managing to keep my skull from whacking against the wood. Saucers of light floated through the blackness of the room; I reached toward them, then gasped, trying to replace the air that the fall had punched from my lungs.

Lucas pawed at my thigh; I grabbed his foot and held on.

The saucers grew smaller. I ran my fingers across my face, expecting to feel blood; finding none.

The glass didn't break, I reminded myself. There wasn't a sound. It wasn't a gun; it was just a light. A flashbulb, maybe.

"Come on, Lucas," I said.

I dragged the blanket from the bed, threw it around my shoulders, and flew down the hall.

Not a flashbulb, I thought. It had lasted too long.

"Move it!" I yelled at him. "Let's go!"

We ran out the front door, down the steps, and around the broken flagstone path to the back of the house. The snow was still coming down; a screen of tiny fast-moving flakes melted when they hit my face. A couple of inches had piled up on the ground.

Lucas snorted in the bushes, clearly intrigued by the scent of something, maybe a person, maybe another dog.

"Who's there?" The back of the house was completely dark; my voice ricocheted off the brick wall and sunk into the snow.

No response. Of course. No sound at all except the wind and the snow-muffled drone of cars over on Huron Avenue.

I ran to the front of the house and looked up and down the block.

Nothing. No car motor, no spinning tires, no shadowy figure weaving in and out of the hedges. Just five or six cars shrouded in snow, a tree branch creaking with the wind, a cat hunched on a porch railing across the street. But now a woman was walking toward me from the corner with a little Toto-type dog on a leash.

I hooked my fingers under Lucas's collar and waited. Maybe she'd been out for a while. Maybe she'd seen someone race around the corner.

The woman came closer.

She wore a mohair cape, a big fringed scarf wrapped around her head and neck, and fur ankle boots.

Her dog yanked at his leash, then reared on his hind legs in delight when he saw Lucas.

"No, Stubb," the woman said. "Behave yourself."

She stopped five feet away and stared at me.

"Did you see anybody?" I asked. "Anybody running down the street? Somebody with a ladder, maybe?"

She couldn't tear her eyes away from my bare feet. Her eyes were light-colored, big, horrified.

"Are you all right?" she said. "Did someone hurt you? Do you need me to take you somewhere?"

Funny, I thought. My feet weren't cold anymore. Maybe it was the adrenaline. Maybe I had a disease.

"No," I said.

I gestured toward the condo.

I'd left the door open.

God, I thought. Whoever it was could have walked on in while I was out back.

"I live here," I said. "I heard someone breaking in. Somebody shone a light through the window at me."

She stepped into the yard.

"Here?" she said. "These windows?"

"No. In the back. At the bedroom windows. They're way high up. They're—"

She reached toward me.

"You're frozen," she said. "You'll get sick."

Her voice came out in puffs of vapor.

I felt a little high, a little sweaty. Whatever phenomenon had been protecting my feet had worn off, and pain stabbed through my ankle bones.

Jesus, I thought. Maybe I did crack my head on the bedroom floor.

The nice lady's face was full of compassion.

Her eyes traveled to the house, then again to me.

"Look," she said. "You can tell me. Is your husband in there? Your boyfriend? You don't have to go back. There are places . . . "

I resisted an impulse to take her up on the offer. Spending the night at a women's shelter didn't seem a half bad deal compared to wondering whether I'd have anymore anonymous visitors.

"No," I said. "That's not it."

She stared at the house again. Her expression had changed

from concern to something more complicated. Pain maybe. Maybe fear.

"Did you buy this place?" she said. "Do you know who—"

She stopped herself.

Of course she knew about Andrea. Everybody around here would.

"No," I said. "I'm a friend."

She walked a few steps away from me, letting Stubb sniff a collapsed garbage bag.

"Are you afraid to go back in?" she asked.

The snow had slowed down to almost nothing.

"No."

"Do you want me to stay with you?"

"No. Thanks anyway. I mean I'm okay, thanks."

"Are you going to call the police?"

"Of course," I said.

Stubb yanked at his leash, boxed his shadow on the snow. He was ready to move.

"All right," she said, then turned back to where she came from.

I ran back inside, knocked the snow from my feet, and yanked on shoes and socks and my jacket. Lucas went nuts when he realized we were going out again; he thought I'd invented a game.

There wasn't a flashlight in the house. No candles, either. No matches. I turned on the bedroom and living room lights, grabbed my camera and flash, and walked back to the flagstone path. The light from the living room was enough to illuminate the side of the house. I could see a mess of kicked-up snow and dents where Lucas had been sniffing around, and my own footprints, melted clear to the ground from the heat of my bare feet, but nothing else—just a silky layer of snow.

I walked to the back of the house.

The bedroom windows contained the light too far up; the ground behind the house stayed dark.

"Heel, boy," I told him. "I don't want you messing up the snow anymore. Stay."

I stared at the windows. If I were planning on breaking into the condo they would have been my last choice. Ten feet off the ground, eight inches narrow, the kind that cranked out. Whoever had shone that light at me must have been on a ladder, or a stool, or on somebody else's shoulders, maybe.

But who could fit through the frame? Whoever it was would have to have the shoulders of a ten-year-old.

Unless he wasn't planning on fitting through the frame at all. After all, until not very long ago the head of my bed was under those windows.

Maybe the idea was that he would break the glass and drop something in. Or point something. A gun, maybe. Or maybe just drop a rock on my head. Like that guy in New York who used to heave concrete blocks off the rooftops on West Forty-fourth Street.

I was dressed warmly now, but my teeth started to chatter. I crouched and took random shots of the ground beneath the windows, stretching the flash, attached to the camera by its cable, out to one side, hoping to supply enough angled light to bring out shadows at the edge of the intruder's footprints. I took the rest of the roll standing up, some while I held the camera at chest level and some at waist level. It didn't even matter if I looked through the viewfinder; I couldn't see anything anyway.

I finished the roll, went back inside, and checked the door locks.

I wished I was back in New York, where my darkroom is next to the kitchen. I'd have to use the school's, or maybe Jack's.

I burrowed back in bed. The high row of windows kept me awake; I decided to avoid an all-night stare-down and dragged the mattress into the other bedroom. It was colder in there, but at least the windows had shades.

Lucas sniffed the edges of the room, baffled by the move.

"Come on to sleep, boy," I said. "Come keep me warm."

13

"WHAT DO YOU THINK JESUS IS DOING RIGHT NOW?"

"Sleeping, I hope," I murmured.

I'd awakened before dawn, then rocked in and out of sleep for a couple of hours, letting whatever came my way on the clock radio wash over me. It mingled with a secretarial work-anxiety dream that was eating at me: in it Fred had come back from Club Med and given me a new word processor—one that didn't have any letters or numbers printed on the keys.

"I think you're ready for it," he said.

On weekday mornings this station served up a call-in recipe show that I was addicted to. On Sundays they transformed to Christian broadcasting.

For a while they were playing hymns that all had the words *blood* or *bloody* in the title: "Washed in the Blood of the Lamb," "The Bloody Fountain," "My Saviour's Blood"—

103

that kind of thing. You could buy the whole tape mail order for only four ninety-five per month.

Now the preacher was revving up.

"I said," he said, "what do you think your savior is doing right now?"

I offed the guy and got ready to take Lucas out around the reservoir.

"Don't worry, honey," I told him. "I won't make you go to a youth fellowship meeting today."

The snow had nearly melted, making the previous night's events seem even more remote and strange than they had in the dark. The thaw from the roof dripped through the downspout by the kitchen window; the trees were bare.

I called Jack.

He couldn't believe it.

"Somebody tried to break in and you didn't call the cops?"

"Stop yelling. I told you—I didn't want to leave the bedroom at first to get to the phone. I didn't want to—"

"But afterward. After the guy was gone didn't you even call and report it?"

What was with him? He'd get so inflamed about things. I'd thought maybe he'd give me a little reassurance. Remind me how good the locks are, maybe.

"What good would that have done? I took pictures. They wouldn't even have done that."

"Are you sure it was the bedroom windows? They're pretty high up. You'd have to be a Celtic to look in one of those. Are you sure you weren't—"

"Dreaming, Jack? Are you kidding? My back is so sore this morning from falling off that crate—"

"Sorry," he said. "It's just really weird."

He paused.

"Do you want to move out here?"

"No, Jack. Thanks anyway."

As soon as I hung up, the phone rang again.

"Lib?"

"Yes?"

"Sam here. Jack's buddy. Hold on, I'm going through an underpass."

Oh great. The car phone.

"I was thinking—" he said.

That's an improvement, I thought.

"I was thinking—" he repeated, "that I was kind of out of line when I was talking to you last week. You know, the crack about your car."

"That's okay. You don't need to apologize."

The line dissolved into static again. I was getting ready to hang up.

"So I wanted to know," he said, "if you could go out to eat with me or something. I usually see the kids Sundays but Patty's parents wanted to take them today."

I got it; he was lonely.

"There's a place," he said, "about halfway between you and me that's pretty good. Huge portions. We bring—" He paused. "We brought the kids there sometimes. They like it. There's pictures of turkeys on the plates."

"No kidding. It sounds okay to me."

And maybe, I thought, he could cast a little light on Andrea. On the stripper pictures, maybe.

He gave me directions.

"Two o'clock, Sammy? Don't start eating until I get there, okay?"

I dragged Lucas out back.

By daylight the yard looked stark and well kept. The only real snow that remained clung in a circle around the base of a spruce tree and at the edges of the house's foundation in the shade of the eaves.

I walked to the back wall. A wobbly wooden fence, built more for ornamental than security reasons, divided Jack and Andrea's lot from the property to the left. The few times I had ventured into the yard before I had assumed it was secured to the brick wall to the rear of the lot. Now I could see that the foot and a half of fencing closest to the wall was rotten and that the end pieces only rested against the wall. When I pushed the slats the fencing bent away, wide enough to allow a person to walk through.

I walked through myself and stepped into an alley that led alongside a school building; there were cutout paper snowflakes taped to the windows. The alley led to the street parallel to Andrea's—an easy exit for my midnight visitor.

Matted leaves, damp from the thawed snow, padded the ground in the alley—not an easy place to rake, I figured. Matted leaves and a gray chunk of rubber.

I picked the thing up.

It was one of those rubber cups that people put on the bottoms of chair legs to keep them from scuffing the floor. About an inch and a half high, about an inch and a half in diameter, and speckled with layers of dried white paint.

It was slit down one side, and bent easily under the pressure of my fingers, which could mean, I thought, that it hadn't been exposed to the outdoors for long. And it had been on top of the matted leaves, not underneath. I pocketed it and headed for the reservoir.

14

THE CRANBERRY SAUCE WAS THE KIND THAT COMES OUT OF THE CAN in one plug. A whole container of it, on a lettuce leaf, just for Sam and me. The Colonial Inn—Families Welcome! had a two-lane salad bar, too, with something I'd never seen at any other salad bar: minimarshmallows. The woman ahead of me glanced furtively over her shoulder, decided I wasn't the kind who would rat on her, and dropped a handful into her pocketbook.

Chickpeas, cottage cheese, canned peaches, bacon bits, Jell-O cubes, cole slaw with crushed pineapple. A little dab'll do ya.

I tried to kill my urge to take pictures of everything—the marshmallow klepto, the family wearing identical football jerseys, the signs on the bathroom doors that said POINTERS and SETTERS—by concentrating on what is for me one of the great riddles of the twentieth century: why are the hardboiled egg slices at salad bars of uniform size?

I returned to the table just as the waitress brought our dinners. They were on huge plates with turkeys painted on them, just like Sam said they would be.

"Great, huh?" he said. "I thought you'd go for this place. Real New England."

He'd been doodling on his paper place mat with a mechanical pencil. Firefly-size fighter jets with broken lines showing the missile trajectories. I'd seen pictures like that before; boys used to draw them in the margins of their notebook paper in third grade.

The waitress poured each of us One Complimentary Glass of Cold Duck. I sipped it and gagged in ladylike fashion. *Lavoris red, stupefying to the palate, suggested with three-bean salad and peanut butter Rice Krispies treats*, the label might say.

Sam swallowed his without coming up for breath. I pushed my glass toward him and he took it with a smile. Then he leaned back in his chair and asked the waitress for a beer.

He was more relaxed than he'd been around Jack. None of the finger-drumming, anyway, and none of the tense looking around the room.

I wondered what the story was there. Was Jack the father figure? The big brother? "Sammy" must be Jack's name for him, I figured. He probably calls him that to be patronizing, to keep the guy in his place even though he makes the deals for the business. I kept reminding myself to call him Sam, what he'd called himself on the phone.

He approached his food the way Lucas does. Head down, single-minded—like he'd bite you if you interrupted him. He didn't even flinch when a lady in a knee-length Pilgrim dress, metal tongs in one hand, running shoes on her feet, pulled a pair of bright orange D-cup-size muffins out of the metal box that hung around her neck and slammed them down on our plates.

"Pumpkin," she said.

"Great."

Sam buttered his. He was wearing a big ring like some guys get at college. Except when I looked at it more closely I could see that it didn't have the name of any school or fraternity engraved on it. Just a pattern of leaves in the gold and some bumps and grooves that, if you didn't look hard, could pass for dates and words. I wondered if it was supposed to be a joke. Something from the back of a comic book: "Be a College Graduate or Just Look Like One."

He was done with his meat already, nearly done with the beer, and partway through the potatoes.

"So where are you from, Sam?"

"What?" he said. "Where am I from?" He looked absently around the room, then came back to his plate.

"Around here," he said. "I guess. I know Patrick from when we were kids. Andrea, too."

He was taking the sugar envelopes out of their tray and reading the information on them while he ate. Birds of North America, I think.

"You guess?"

"Yeah," he said. "I guess. I mean I've lived other places, too. I was in the army for a while."

"Are your folks still around?"

He'd cleared his plate right down to the picture and was eyeing mine. I pushed it toward him.

"My folks?" he said. "No."

He finished my green beans, then sopped up the gravy with a piece of bread.

I wondered why he'd bothered asking me to have dinner with him. No small talk, no questions, the shortest answers possible. Like a police officer escorting a nonviolent offender from one correctional facility to another and stopping for lunch on the way. I wouldn't have been surprised if he'd pulled out a *TV Guide* and started to read it.

The waitress cleared the table and brought us slices of pecan pie with whipped topping and our own thermal pitcher of coffee. I poured the coffee, Sam ate the pie, the baby at the next table smeared mashed potatoes around on her highchair tray.

"So Sam, how about those Red Sox?" I asked him before I realized I was in the wrong season.

He looked at me blandly.

"Huh?"

"I mean, how about this weather? Snow last night, sun this afternoon . . . "

"Uh huh," he said. "The weather."

Halfway through the second piece of pie he finally stopped eating. His eyes stopped looking empty and hungry; now they had a nearly reflective look that I hadn't seen before.

"I guess," he said, "she must of felt sorry for me."

"Who?"

"Andrea."

What brought on this outburst of intimacy? Maybe the combination of cold duck and beer had blasted his brain circuitry. His cheeks were glowing.

"Because my dad was dead," he continued. "I never thought about it before, but I guess that must've been it. Their parents were dead too, you know—Patrick and Andrea's. The mother and the father both.

"She threw a party for us once. For Patrick and me—when we graduated from high school. Somebody she knew had a pool and let her, you know, borrow it. They were out of town or something. She let us invite whoever we wanted. Girls and everything. She got all this food—a barbecue grill, drinks, everything."

He wiped at the side of his nose with the back of his hand.

"You would have thought we were her own kids or something. You know?"

We all stayed kids, I thought. Me, Jack, everybody back at school. We all stayed kids for a long time and Andrea turned into an adult overnight.

Now he was stacking the little sealed cups of creamer on top of one another. The guy always had to be doing something. Eating, drawing, making plans.

"She had on a white bathing suit," he said.

He frowned while he said it, then smiled a little.

"That's funny. I only just remembered it now. She was wearing a white bathing suit at the party. I remember because I never saw one before until then."

And she probably looked drop-dead beautiful, I thought. Andrea looked drop-dead beautiful in anything. Bathrobe and flip-flops, threadbare jeans and army surplus jacket, lawyer garb. The kid had seen white bathing suits before, I thought. He'd just never seen one on Andrea.

He flushed.

"I never met another woman like her," he said. "She had, I don't know, how would you say it? She had class. She was a classy lady. How she dressed. How she talked. You know? She was the kind of girl a guy like I—"

He pleated the paper muffin wrapper into a little rectangle, then wiped his mouth with it.

"Patty," he said, "my wife—or whatever she is now—she used to get really mad when I'd talk about Andrea. She never wanted to do anything with Jack and her. You know, that's another thing that really makes me mad. What was Andrea supposed to do? Make herself look ugly so Patty wouldn't get jealous? Make herself sound dumb?"

He poured another cup of coffee. He wasn't really talking to me now; he was just talking. If I'd gotten up and left he probably wouldn't have noticed.

"Andrea and me," he said, "we understood each other. We both, you know, wanted to do things. Get ahead. Travel. Be somebody. Somebody people notice when you walk into a room. Like they want to take your coat off and hang it up for you. Talk to you. Listen to you."

Coffee sloshed out of the mug when he set it down, but he didn't notice.

"That's another thing about Andrea," he said. "The way she listened to what a guy was saying. She always listened to me. Even when we were kids."

I wondered if she listened or if she was just glazed over the way I was now.

He leaned closer toward me.

"You know," he said, "sometimes I used to think what if—"

"What if what?"

"Nothing."

"What?"

"What if I'd met Andrea before Jack did? You know, if I'd been older. Maybe we could of got together, you know? What a team."

"Yeah," I said. "That would really have been something, wouldn't it?"

The Pilgrim waitress was walking around the room giving helium balloons to all the little kids. I had a fleeting fantasy that she might come to our table and tie one to Sam's wrist, but she didn't. He was in a fog, fantasizing, I guess, about life with Andrea.

I'd put the envelope of stripper pictures in my bag, on the

floor by my feet. I didn't want to leave them in the condo, didn't want anybody who didn't know Andrea bumping into them by accident. The corner of the envelope was rubbing against the back of my calf.

"Do you know if Andrea had a camera? If she ever took any pictures?"

He emptied the coffee carafe into his cup.

"I don't think so," he said. "She was too busy. She probably didn't even know how to use one. She worked too hard. She wouldn't have had the time."

Of course that's how it was. After RIT Andrea had never looked back. How could she have? Taking care of her brother, all that studying, the job at the library . . .

He stirred some creamer in.

"Except," he said, "she gave Patrick a camera once and I think it used to be hers. We were kids, you know. It was Patrick's birthday or something. Maybe we were fourteen or fifteen."

"What did he do with it?"

"Do with it?" He snorted, laughed, then covered his eyes with his hand for a moment, as though he could hardly bear the scene that his memory was retrieving.

"Do with it?" he said again. "He took it over to Spy Pond— they had that apartment in Arlington then—and dropped it by mistake in the water. I was with him."

His voice grew quieter.

"The water wrecked it and he didn't have the money to get it fixed. I don't know if he ever told Andrea. He felt real bad."

"You never saw her with another camera? Taking snap-shots maybe? Using Jack's darkroom?"

He pushed his chair away from the table and folded his arms across his chest.

"Uh-uh," he said. "Not Andrea. She hardly ever came out to the barn. She said Jack's mom's dogs made her eyes itch.

113

She lived at her office most of the time. She had to. Otherwise she would never have made partner."

He started doodling again. This time it was three-dimensional letters with shadows behind them.

"So how come," he said, "you want to know about her taking pictures?"

"I don't know," I said. "No, I guess I do know. Andrea and I—that is, Jack and Andrea and I—went to school in Rochester together for a while. She was a photographer then. A really good one. And then her parents were killed. That's when she came back here."

"To take care of Patrick."

"Right. And decided to become a lawyer. I think she had it in her mind that she had to do something that would give her some financial security, since she would be taking care of Patrick. He was just little, I think. Ten or eleven. I think she knew she'd be the one to send him to college."

"He never went."

"I don't know anything about him," I said. "What's he like?"

He exhaled again, this time louder.

"Patrick," he said.

"Yeah, Patrick."

"He's got a temper."

"A bad one?"

"Pretty bad," he said. "Almost like Jack's."

"I didn't know Jack had a temper."

He chewed the side of his thumb.

"Jack doesn't show it a lot. He kind of simmers for a while. A long while. Maybe he doesn't like the way I handled a meeting or something. But he doesn't tell me right off. He just sits on it. For a long time. Months maybe. And then—BAM!—he's yelling and throwing stuff around and I'm trying to remember what it was I did in the first place because it was a really long time ago. You know what I mean?"

114

I did. My dad was like that for a while when we were kids. It made us all real nervous, like when you're waiting for one of those spring-loaded suction-cup dolls to launch off a tabletop. Except every day and all day long.

"Patrick's like that, too?"

"Kind of. It's more like Jack brings it out in him. I think the problem is that Jack sees all the bad stuff that's in himself in Patrick, and it makes him crazy. Patrick never acts like that around me."

Sam was looking morose.

"Do you see Patrick much?"

"Not as much as I'd like to. I've got kids, you know. And it makes Jack . . . "

His voice tapered away.

"It makes Jack mad if you see Patrick?"

"Yeah," he said. "It does."

He lowered his voice again. "Patrick's starting up his own landscaping business. That's what I started telling Jack in the barn when you were there. And I . . . "

His eyes darted around the room, as though he thought Jack might be there, disguised as a Pilgrim waitress or something.

"And I'm thinking of going in with him."

"And you're afraid it will make Jack mad? How old are you, anyway? Why should you have to worry—"

He motioned me to lower my voice, even though I wasn't speaking loudly.

"It's not just that," he said. "It's a lot of things. I owe Jack. He brought me in as his partner, gave me a lot of responsibility. And we were doing pretty well for a while there, with the timer switch we were making. I made that deal myself, you know? We did great there for a while. I feel like I owe him. Like this wouldn't be a good time to run out on him. Not with Andrea just gone, too."

This was killing him. The guy wanted to be on the Cape with Patrick, starting over.

"So why don't you—"

"That's not everything," he interrupted. "Part of it is that Jack's pissed at Patrick because he and Andrea paid for all his drug and alcohol rehab, and then Andrea left him some insurance money, and Jack thinks Patrick ought to use it to pay him back."

"Was it a lot of money?"

He thought for a bit.

"Yeah," he said. "Pretty much a lot of money. A couple a hundred grand. You know, Jack and Andrea got along pretty well, but when it came to money—" He rolled his eyes skyward.

"They had a tough time?"

"Yeah, well, Andrea wasn't into risk."

"Like Jack's business."

"Like Jack's business," he said. "She had different ideas about money. She had to. She had to pinch and save everywhere to take care of her and Patrick. It was the way she was. I used to get on Jack about it."

He shook his head. "But boy," he said, "Jack could have used some of that insurance money last year, funding the Snake Eye."

"So where did he get it?"

He shrugged. "He raised it somehow. That's not my end of the business. He raised it somehow. He always does."

We walked out to the parking lot. The sun had disappeared again, a breeze had kicked up, and a father was trying to stuff his kids' helium balloons into the backseat of his car.

"So, Sam," I said, opening my Rabbit, "what do you think of the idea that Andrea was in love with that guy LeClair when she died?"

He wouldn't meet my eyes; he reached over the windshield to pick some dead leaves out of my wipers.

"I don't know," he finally said. "At first I thought no, she would never, but—"

He messed with my side mirror.

"But what?" I said again.

"Nothing."

"Come on, tell me. I want to know. I need to know."

I had caught him at a vulnerable time, I realized. Holidays coming up. His marriage in smithereens. No family. Just finished consoling himself with a stranger and cold duck.

"Patty," he said. "She has a cousin who worked at the law firm Andrea was at. She was a bookkeeper, I think. Maybe collections."

"So what did she say?"

His face was pink. He looked around the lot, then leaned closer toward me.

"Don't ever tell Jack this," he said. "It would kill him. Or he'd kill me."

"What?"

"Patty's cousin said it was all over the firm. Andrea was in love with the guy. And Patty says it happens all the time. She's seen it on TV. On one of those talk shows. Sometimes they fall in love with guys on death row. Can you believe it? I guess they just go kind of crazy. You know. Temporary insanity or something."

His voice was flippant, but his face was pained.

"You think Andrea went crazy?"

His eyes grew bigger.

"They do, you know," he said. "Sometimes."

"They" being womankind, I guess.

"My mom did," he said, "for a while."

"Your mom."

"She's okay now," he said. "Pretty much."

"Pretty much," I repeated. "Okay. I mean, that's good."

I got in the car. He stood there, staring, looking like he was about to say something, but not letting it out.

"What is it, Sam? Is something wrong?"

He stared for a little longer, then stuffed his hands in his pockets.

"Yeah," he said. "I think you ought to get a new car."

15

JACK'S DARKROOM, AT THE BACK OF THE BARN, WAS A MESS. I SPENT forty-five minutes wiping the counters clean, dusting the enlarger, washing the coffee cups in the sink, trying to find a container of developing solution that hadn't expired a long time ago. It ticked me off. Slovenly housekeeping I can take. Dirty refrigerators, bathtubs with scum in them, even. But a filthy darkroom? Who could work in this? Darkrooms should be shrines to order, temples of efficiency and convenience, places where you could splice genes if you had to. I cleaned out the developing tanks and searched the barn for a towel to dry them.

The entire place was a mess. Both beds unmade, piles of design plans and manila files on the tables, a dozen cameras in different stages of disembowelment here, there, and everywhere. For some reason it pained me to see so many cameras in pieces. I patted mine reassuringly. No way I'd let him get his hands on *you*.

Last night's interrupted sleep and the meal earlier in the day at the Colonial had taken their toll; I was tired, leaden-feeling, on edge. I opened the door at the back of the room, expecting to find a utility closet—more developer maybe, a broom. Instead I walked into another room, a little larger than the darkroom, and windowless.

I groped for a light switch but couldn't find one, then waited for the light from the darkroom to filter into the room and for my eyes to adjust to the dimness. There we were: more boxes, some half-built utility shelving, an abandoned exercise bike, a—I drew back against the wall, a shudder of sick fear seizing the center of my chest.

Something was hanging from the ceiling. Something heavy and oblong, hanging on a rope. Something that I couldn't make out because it was in the vaguest penumbra of light from the darkroom.

"Jack! Jack!"—the word was a dry heave.

I stepped into darkness toward the object, reached to touch it. It was flat, smooth, hard, with sewn seams. It was a punching bag.

"Idiot," I hissed at myself.

I backed into the darkroom, and waited for the sound of the blood banging in my head to disappear.

A punching bag. Was it Sam's? Was it Jack's? I had a hard time thinking about Jack going at it. He'd registered CO during Vietnam, hadn't he?

I went about my business of developing and printing the pictures from the yard, thinking next week's lectures through at the same time.

Damn. The film was a wipeout. I'd set the distance wrong in the dark. No footprints, no ladder prints, no nothing. Just frame-to-frame blur.

The door screeched open and Jack's mother stepped in.

"Hi," I said. "Jack said I—"

"Could use his darkroom. Of course. He told me."

She looked three inches taller than she had when I'd seen her limping around the field with her mattock. She'd consolidated the weird-looking buns over each ear into just one at the back of her head. And instead of her wrung-out cardigan she wore a tweed jacket with velvet lapels.

What did Jack say had been wrong with her? Hip replacement surgery? Cataracts? Whatever her medical problem had been she looked okay now.

"I've made some coffee," she said. "You need a break from your work. Jack always does at this time of day."

I resisted an urge to click my heels and salute her. "Sure," I said. "Thanks. I like coffee anytime." Lucas sidled up next to her and beat his tail against the floor.

She patted his head.

"Aren't you a lovely creature," she said. "My, my, my."

Her manners were so good she didn't ask me what had happened to Lucas's leg even though I knew she wanted to. Everyone always wants to.

Lucas slobbered on her hand.

"Come meet my Briskit," she said. "And Swift. We'll have some treats. They're delicious."

I was a little excited until I realized she was talking to Lucas, not me.

We followed her outside and into the kitchen; she motioned for Lucas and me to continue to the living room.

The place was decorated Yankee-style: threadbare rugs; lots of fireplace equipment; no visible magazines.

A yellow dog slept on one sofa, a black dog on the other. They ignored Lucas and I felt a little hurt for him.

Family portraits hung over the mantel—

Wait a minute.

I walked closer.

They were family portraits all right, but of dogs. Framed needlepoint portraits of springer spaniels, black labs, a collie, a pathetic-looking Pekingese on a plaid pillow that had tassels at the corners.

The framed photographs on the sideboard were of dogs, too. No Jack, no long-dead Mr. Hale, no pictures from Andrea and Jack's wedding, no big family reunion at the beach. Just dogs. Dogs sitting in boats, dogs with big sticks in their mouths, dogs with Christmas bows around their necks.

Jack's mother set a tray on the wooden chest next to the sofa. It had two cups of black coffee on it—one with a big chip out of the lip—and a saucer filled with Milk-Bone dog biscuits.

She passed me the unchipped cup.

"Thanks, Mrs. Hale."

I scalded my tongue with the first sip. She must have double-nuked it in the microwave.

"Jane B.," she said.

"Jane B."

She took a long draft from hers without flinching. I noticed for the first time that one of her eyelids hung lower than the other. Maybe she'd had a stroke. Maybe that's what Jack had said.

We stared out the window at the field. The ground was hard-looking, rocky, deadly still; the sky was gray and flat. If the view were a photograph I'd say I should have left it in the developer a little longer. Then again, I'd probably never have taken it in the first place.

"I understand," she said, "that Jack is enjoying"—she finally located the word—"distaff company again. He speaks highly of you."

Distaff company?

I couldn't think of anything appropriately stilted and polite to respond with, so I stayed quiet.

She snapped her fingers. The big yellow dog poured himself off the sofa and trotted over. She shoved a biscuit into his mouth.

"Good boy," she said.

She watched him eat it, then returned her gaze to me.

"He—" she said, "Jack, that is, has taken his wife's death poorly."

Suddenly her bad eyelid shot up, the way defectively rolled window shades do sometimes.

I tried not to gawk at it.

Poorly? I thought. How else are you supposed to take your wife's murder?

"My side of the family," she said, "takes things in stride."

Of course, I thought. You're supposed to take it *in stride*.

She aimed her gaze at me for a long, long moment. I would have confessed if I'd had anything to confess.

"And we are not," she said, "strangers to misfortune."

I prepared myself for the litany of gruesome family events: the stillborn baby, the small plane that crashed in Maine, the dive into the empty swimming pool that claimed the older brother, maybe?

But no. We had a Yankee here. No such indulgence.

"Jack's father was too soft with him," she said. "He never disciplined consistently and often too long after the event. The boy was never sure of his boundaries. I took on that task."

I imagined Jack as a toddler, his mother fastening him to a run in the backyard, a bowl of water at one end, a rubber bone at the other.

"I am compelled to tell you," she said, "that Jack is a complicated boy. He needs to be handled carefully. But I also want you to know that you have my blessing."

What was she talking about?

She took a Milk-Bone from the saucer, dunked it in her coffee, and bit it in half.

I gagged. I know the story about Queen Victoria drinking out of her finger bowl to be gracious just because a visiting dignitary drank out of his, but I guess I'm not the gracious type.

"Well thanks," I said. "Thanks for everything. I've really got to be—"

A little bird dive-bombed against the window and dropped to the ground.

"God!" I said. "Poor thing! Don't you think we should—"

The grounded bird collected itself in a flutter of feathers and dead leaves, then flew off again.

"I think," I said, "you ought to pull the curtains this time of day. Then they won't see their reflections. That's what they go after, their reflections—"

She ate the rest of the dog biscuit, put her cup back on the tray, and rose to see me out the door. Her bad eyelid quivered, then dropped.

"The birds," she said, "know how to take care of themselves."

16

THE EARLY BIRD, I REMINDED MYSELF, GETS THE WORM. BUT ONLY, that is, if she has a big cup of coffee first.

The coffee machines in the Darling and Ueland kitchen were empty. I rummaged through the drawers, looking for vacuum-packed envelopes of preground beans. Spoons, Sweet'n Low, a case of nondairy creamer, a bottle of Maalox, discount coupons for buying more Sweet'n Low . . .

"Penny Kincaid please call Mrs. Cox. Penny Kincaid."

Funny, I thought—there's somebody else here named Kincaid. Maybe I've got a cousin—

My vision was blurred. My neurotransmitters were shooting off sparks. I wouldn't even be able to figure out how to turn the computer on, let alone manage to do a paragraph indent.

I looked under the sink. Praise Jesus. A big box of gold foil packets. I ripped one open with my teeth and dumped the contents into the filter.

"Penny!"

Darthea Cox stood in the doorway, her eyes wide with panic.

Hey, wait a minute, I thought. She's right. *I'm* Penny.

"Yes, Darthea?"

I wanted to say, What in the world are you doing here, Darthea? I got here forty-five minutes early so I could have some peace and quiet to— Actually, to snoop in, but I couldn't tell her that.

"I've got two clients in the Ueland Room, Penny, and there's no coffee, the table's a mess, and the stapler is empty. I told you Friday night to get the room ready for today."

Liar, I didn't say to her. Did not.

She yanked a tray from the top of the refrigerator and started dumping cups and saucers onto it. Her hands were shaking; her hair was wet from her morning shower; her complexion was the color of the rubber Resusci-Anne doll they make you blow into in CPR class.

She looked at the coffee machine's empty pots with horror.

"Where's Marie?" she said. "Marie starts those at seven! What's going on?"

"Marie is probably busy," I said. "Fred is on vacation."

She lifted the tray cockeyed; the dishes slid to one end. I took it from her.

"Are you okay?"

"Of course I'm okay," she barked. "If you'd only—"

I poured tap water into the top of the coffee machine. Darthea dumped sugar cubes into a saucer. Half of them fell to the floor. She scraped them into a pile with her foot. She was wearing one navy pump and one black one, but she was so strung out she didn't notice.

"It's Katherine Spank," she said. "She wants to reneg on

126

the settlement. You know—we did the agreement on Friday. She called me at three this morning and told me to tell Mark Adler she'd changed her mind. *Changed her mind!* She knows I can't do that. She authorized me to settle and I did."

She picked up the little pitcher I'd just filled with milk and put it back into the refrigerator. I took it out again and put it on the tray.

The woman was worse than rattled; she was like somebody who'd just had brake failure on FDR Drive at rush hour.

"Do you think," I said, "that she's going to pretend that you settled without her permission?"

Her eyes darted to the doorway. No one was there.

"You think so, too?" she said.

"I don't know. You just seem kind of nervous."

"She's nuts," she whispered. "She's a complete neurotic. I don't know how Andrea put up with her. I'll be dead in a week."

Please don't say that, I started to say, but she was racing down the hall.

I spent the morning filing—my nails that is—and answering the phone. I have a very nice phone manner, which I developed the summer I was nine years old. That was when my father made me pretend to be his secretary when he was Making Good Money in his Spare Time at Home by selling phony rare coins by mail. I modeled my voice on Della Street's. Husky but crisp. Sexy but practical.

Darthea called from the conference room and commanded me to cancel all of her morning appointments.

Every half hour or so Schuyler Kreps, who was spending the morning locked in his office, buzzed me on the intercom.

"Clear your decks," he'd say. "Don't let anybody else give you anything to do. This is going to be huge."

Lorna was outrageously busy in the next cubicle. Her

phone rang constantly; the two lawyers she worked for popped alternately out of their office doors every five minutes, like figures on a Bavarian clock.

I escaped at one for lunch. There was a big semiabandoned shopping mall behind the Jordan Marsh department store. I bought an Orange Julius there and ate it outside on the pedestrian mall. A guy tried to sell me a phony Rolex watch from a selection safety-pinned to the inside of his coat. A man with matted hair, wearing a woman's coat, knelt in the center of the sidewalk, holding out a Kentucky Fried Chicken tub with a sign taped on it that said HELP ME.

Just like home. Except if I were in New York some guy in a fancy three-piece suit would be banging a street lamp with his briefcase and talking to himself.

I put the change from my Orange Julius into the tub.

"Excuse me," I said. "Where's the Combat Zone?"

The man turned slightly on his haunches, peeled his thumb from the rim of the bucket, and gestured down Washington Street.

"Careful," he said. "Jesus will see you."

"That's okay," I said.

17

LIVE NUDE BABY-SITTERS, THE SIGN SAID.

"Better than dead nude baby-sitters," I muttered, trying to relax. I get as sentimental as the next mass-media operative about most First Amendment issues—say, the right not to squeal on your sources and the right to make fun of politicians—but I get tense about porn palaces. Octavia might say that I take the idea *too personally.*

TOPLESS GIRLS NIGHTLY.

I slid one of the stripper photographs from Andrea's partway out of the envelope.

The dressing room in the picture was just below street level, and the window, which was high on the wall, was covered with a protective grating. I traced the pattern of the iron with my finger: nothing very fancy, just six twisted vertical bars with a diamond shape anchored between the center pair.

I shoved the picture back in my bag and prowled the block, looking for the grate.

Nothing doing. Six straight vertical bars here; eight straight vertical bars there; now seven twisted bars with arrowheads molded at the tops; a bunch of S-shaped bars that bulged away from the window—but no diamonds. I walked around the block, then a second block, then crossed the street and repeated the routine.

The Zone was dead. Not like Times Square, where the action moves around the clock. Here there were padlocks on the doors, CLOSED signs in the windows, trash from the night before heaped on the sidewalk. A guy in an orange sweat suit was taping big X's out of masking tape on the front window of his Ginseng Specialties shop. Maybe, I thought, it's some kind of spell to keep intruders out.

In the forty minutes since I'd left the office the temperature had dropped so far so fast that my inner ears ached, and the sky was spritzing snow.

The flakes that came down were widely spaced and taking zany trajectories, repelled by the warm air rising from the grates in the sidewalk.

There was a fishy taste in the air. I stuck out my tongue and caught a snowflake; it tasted fishy, too.

Must be because of the harbor, I thought, even though I wasn't sure how far away from the harbor the Combat Zone was. That's what everybody around here said when the air smelled funny. *Must be the harbor.*

I crossed the street to the only open store. MANNY'S JOKE SHOP it said on the sign, with a crude cartoonlike drawing of a fat guy looking real happy even though his cigar just blew up in his face. The window looked like it was decorated by somebody from a work-release program for sex offenders.

The backdrop was masks—the kind you pull on over your

head: King Kong heads, giant rubber baby heads, a fur chicken head with a rubber tongue hanging out of its rubber beak—standing sentry over the holiday feature: a ceramic nativity scene that included a statue of Santa Claus praying over the baby Jesus, who was nestled on a mess of white fiberfill batting like they stuff cheap pillows with. An electric train looped around the setup, stopping occasionally to blink its headlights and grind its wheels through a snag in the fiberfill. The front of the window was littered with phony beer and pop cans—the kind that are made out of Mylar so you can surprise your friends with how easily they smash against your forehead. The weirdest stuff—huge plastic breasts and rear ends that you could strap over your own—hung discreetly at the sides of the windows.

I lifted my camera and backed up, trying to avoid the glare in the glass from the lighting inside the store.

A guy stepped out of the next doorway—hefty, purple-cheeked, wearing a powder blue vinyl jacket and a red plaid beret and carrying a roll of masking tape. "Hey!" he said. "Cut it out. I tole you before. You got no business doing that!"

He reached for my camera; I backed off.

His nose was huge and pockmarked; his hands were as big as dustpans. He was breathing hard.

"I tole you," he said. "You gotta have permission from the owner to do that, and you're not getting it. You have to pay to do that. It's copyright. I ought to know."

I slipped my camera into my jacket.

"Okay," I said. "I'll remember that."

He looked at me more closely. A visual frisk, up and down and all over, like guys do in Italy.

"Hey," he said. "You ain't the same—"

"The same what?"

He didn't answer.

Crevices ran from the corners of his mouth to the sides of

his nose. Deep ones—like the lines on a ventriloquist's dummy. He spat on the sidewalk.

"You ain't undercover, huh?"

I thought that would be a good thing to be right then, so I didn't say anything.

"I tole you," he said. "I'm in compliance. In compliance!"

He stripped a length of tape from the roll. My heart froze.

"Get out of here," he said.

I toyed with the idea of saying "It's a free country"—one of my father's favorite lines—decided against it, and walked off in the direction I'd come from. Halfway down the block I turned around and watched the guy disappear into the doorway he'd stepped out of. Then I walked back to the joke shop.

This time I went straight in. One side of the store was lined with cardboard boxes filled with the gizmos that get advertised in the back of comic books: pretend ice cubes with dead flies in them, foaming sugar cubes, joy buzzers, severed hands, phony barf.

Somebody had dropped a wallet on the floor. I reached down to pick it up and it leapt away.

"Gottcha!"

A tiny woman, seventy maybe, wearing a nice wool skirt, a blouse with a Peter Pan collar, and a cardigan fastened at the neck with a diaper pin, stepped out from behind the counter and started to giggle. The wallet dangled from her hand on a piece of fishing line.

"Yeah," I said. "Got me all right."

"Kids love it," she said.

A doorway behind the counter had a sign that said ADULTS ONLY. The lady watched me take in the sign, then stepped aside to let me through.

"Are you looking for something special?"

She had a pleasant, eager-to-please look on her face.

"Uh, maybe. Early Christmas shopping, I guess you could say. I have to mail a lot of things out of town."

She brightened.

"We gift wrap," she said.

Crotchless underpants with cap guns in holsters on the sides, leather underpants with zippers on them; vibrators with happy faces on them. It was like the collective unconscious of the Looney Tunes gang. Like Elmer Fudd meets Hannibal Lecter.

"Remember," the lady said, "something special for you means something special for him!"

I feigned interest in a lady's maid getup. Black sateen top, white lace cap, apron so small it could double as a pot holder.

"I don't know," I said, "the apron doesn't seem big enough."

"That's okay," she winked.

She took what looked like a toy toilet from a shelf and fooled around with the handle.

It was a radio.

"Cute," she said, smiling. She set it on the counter. "Let's get the word on the storm."

"Really? We're getting a storm?" My morning recipe show didn't do weather.

"Don't you know? Any time now! It's the big one, that's what they're saying! As big as seventy-eight!"

I remembered seventy-eight. That was when you could ski down Fifth Avenue, if you had skis. It was unbelievably scary and gorgeous. And the city absolutely quiet because the cars couldn't go.

Talk radio came out of the little toilet, not the weather. The voices were puny and choked with static.

"Seventy-eight," the lady said. "Thirty-four people killed in Massachusetts. Most of them out on one-twenty-eight. Froze in their cars. Or monoxide got them. I always bring an orange in the car in bad weather. You should, too."

I tucked the little apron back into its box, then pulled the pictures out of my bag.

"Yes, dear?" she said. "Don't be so shy."

"I'm looking," I said, "for something a little different. Like these."

I pointed at the stripper's tassels.

"Maybe," I said, "I'm in the wrong kind of shop. Maybe a millinery store would be better. What do you—"

She frowned, squinted, pulled a pair of glasses out of her sleeve, and put them on.

"Why my goodness!" she said. "Is she your mother? I see the resemblance. I certainly do. I see it right through—"

She brushed my jaw with her fingertips.

"No," I said. "She's not my mother. I took these pictures and then I lost the lady's address. Hey, maybe you . . . "

She clicked her tongue against the roof of her mouth.

"Let's see," she said. "Oh yes. She worked at Gillfooley's." She tipped her head, reconsidering. "No, no, not at all. She worked at the Moonstone—no! The Pussycat!—when the Pussycat was still there, that is. It's gone now. Completely gone. I heard she was sick for a while there—"

She looked at me darkly and lowered her voice—

"She had to have her organs removed."

She took the picture again.

"Of course," she said, "it might not be her at all."

She tipped her head in the other direction.

"No," she said. "I don't believe it is the same woman after all!"

I had another idea.

I reached into my wallet and took out the old photo booth picture of Andrea and me.

"See her?" I said, pointing at Andrea. "Have you ever seen her around?"

She fooled with her glasses again. Off, on, down near the end of her nose.

"Why I believe I may have," she said.

"Where? When? Can you remember?"

The radio went dead. The lady slammed it against the counter but it wouldn't come back.

"Not to mention," she said, "the women having babies."

"What?"

"In seventy-eight," she said. "Couldn't get out of their houses, poor things. Doctors had to tell them what to do over the phone. One girl's husband had to cut her open with a steak knife. Imagine . . . "

She looked at me. "You look pale," she said. "Oh, I'm sorry. You're not pregnant, are you? Because if you are . . . "

"No," I said, "just doing some shopping."

I picked out a feather boa for Claire, a pack of Chewing Gum So Hot It Will Bring Tears to Your Eyes for that special someone, I wasn't sure yet who, and put them next to the cash register.

The woman reached under the counter and brought out a white, flattish cardboard box. She took off the lid and turned the box toward me. The tassels were faded, like something you'd see hanging from your grandmother's drapes.

I picked two rose-colored ones.

"That's nice," she said, "when they're the same color."

There was a thud at the back of the store.

"That's Manny," the woman said. "Coming in the basement door. Let me ask him. He'll know. He's my brother. He knows everything. He's been taping up the windows for the storm. So if the glass breaks it will all stick together."

She yelled down the stairs.

"Manny! Remember that girl who was around here taking pictures? The one you threw out? The blond?"

F-words floated up the staircase.

"No, Manny, she's not back."

More curses.

"He doesn't know," she said. "But she was around here a lot for a while. Nice girl. Nice build. She used to bring me a cup of coffee."

"When was that?"

She took a handkerchief out of her sleeve and rubbed her nose with it.

"Oh my," she said. "A year ago. Maybe two years ago. My memory's not what it used to be. Not since—"

She leaned close to me again.

"My husband passed on."

"I see," I said. "That's too bad."

I took the picture back.

"Did the girl say why she was taking pictures?"

She shrugged. "I don't know," she said. "Trying out her camera, maybe. I don't remember. I wouldn't have remembered if she'd stuffed it in my ear and sewed it up. Nice girl, though."

She glanced toward the back of the store. Manny-land.

"Some of us thought so, anyway," she said.

What in the world had Andrea been up to? Collecting evidence—for what? Wasn't that the sort of thing she would have hired a detective to do?

"Did she ever have anybody with her?"

"The little blond?"

"Yes. Her. Did she ever bring anybody with her?"

"Oh no. I don't think so."

She rang up my purchases and stuffed them into a bag.

"I used to think—" she said, then stopped.

"Think what?"

"That she wanted to dance. She could have, you know."

She handed me the bag.

"You'll need some wig tape," she said.

"What?"

"Wig tape. You never used it? It's double-sided. For the tassels, dear. It holds real nice."

"Thanks."

I turned to go.

"Hey . . . " she said.

"What?"

She walked me to the door.

"Do you want to be a dancer?" she said.

"Maybe," I said.

She put her face so close to mine the mentholyptus fumes from her cough drop stung my eyes.

"Don't let them tell you you're too flat-chested," she said. "It's not true."

I opened the door into a whiteout of snow.

"Thanks," I said. "I'll remember that."

18

I GOT IN THE ELEVATOR JUST AS EVERYBODY ELSE IN THE BUILDING seemed to be leaving.

"Snow day!" somebody yelled. A couple of people threw hats in the air. "All right!"

"Hey Penny! Turn around! Marie's sending us home!"

It was a secretary I'd never talked with before, but I'd seen her in the bathroom.

Lorna broke away from the crowd.

Her face was tight.

"You better get up there," she said. "Schuyler's having a fit. He was talking about calling the agency, but I covered for you. Don't even go to the bathroom. Just move it."

The secretarial stations were empty, but most of the lawyers seemed to be in their offices.

I slipped into my seat and tried not to look too guilty. After all, I was only—

"—an hour late!"

Schuyler smiled tensely over the counter at me.

"I don't even want to know," he said. "Buying makeup, getting your nails done—do me a favor. Don't tell me about it."

"Sorry," I said.

"Okay," he said. "But you've got a hell of a lot of work to get out."

He dropped a yellow legal pad onto my desktop.

"Notices of eviction," he said. "Muldoon wants to go ahead and unload the building. We've got to get these out certified by the end of the day. Got it?"

"Got it."

My chair, which had wheels, was on a Lucite mat so it wouldn't slow down on the carpet. I lifted my feet from the ground to yank off my boots and the chair rolled backward. I pulled the chair forward again, lifted my feet up, and the chair took off again.

"Hey," I said. "What's this? The building's swaying or something."

"That's nothing," he said. "Look at this!"

He set his pencil on my desk and it rolled off.

"Great," I said. "The building is swinging back and forth and we're twenty-eight floors up."

"Oh yeah?" he said. "You better be glad this building swings back and forth. It's supposed to. Otherwise it would just crack up."

"She's right, Schuyler. This isn't a safe place to be in a storm. You ought to go home right now, Penny, like everybody else."

It was Darthea, handing me time sheets.

"Marie sent all the staff home, Schuyler," she said. "And

I'm going to be out of here in ten minutes. It's just not safe. The Pike will be awful."

Kreps watched her walk to her office and mouthed "the Pike will be awful," at her back, with a prissy face, the way a bad child would.

"Yeah, yeah, yeah," he said, on his way back to the desk. "There's not going to be any storm. The weather guys just like to get everybody excited."

My computer screen went blank. Then a message blinked on.

"Back up all documents. Building management says tape your windows. See me for tape. Marie."

Another message followed:

"See me for beer. TMJ."

Then: "Six feet of packed powder at Mt. Snow. Three more today. Kowabunga!"

The place was going haywire.

I started getting worried about Lucas. He'd never been in a snowstorm by himself before. What if the heat went out in the condo? Good thing the dog walker was coming in. When did she say she'd be there? Three? Three-thirty? She sounded so businesslike. So dependable.

I formatted my first certificate of eviction. Nice and easy. Not as bad as they looked—the same form over and over, just the addresses were different.

Asterisks blasted all over the screen.

"Management has ordered that we evacuate the building. Marie."

Followed by: "JSM has ordered five large Domino's pizzas. JSM."

Followed by: "Videotapes of former associate Carl Clonus practicing opening arguments will be shown in the Darling Room at five-fifteen."

Darthea was at my desk again. She wore a white rabbit fur

hat and wound her scarf around her mouth as she spoke so I
could barely hear her.

"Here," she said. "Shine viss."

Sign this.

The piece of paper said:

> Whereas, the Channel Five weather report has
> predicted a severe snowstorm starting today at
> midafternoon, and whereas Darthea Cox has ordered
> me to leave the Darling and Ueland premises and I
> have refused to leave the premises, I will hold
> Darthea Cox harmless as to any injuries, including
> but not limited to physical and emotional injuries
> that I may suffer as the result of my refusal to leave
> the building.
>
> Signed under the pains
and penalties of perjury.

———————————————

Penny Kincaid

"Are you kidding?"

"No. You're the only secretary here, and I don't want anybody saying that I made you stay to work."

"Well, I don't know, but . . . "

"Don't sign it. On the advice of your attorney."

It was Schuyler Kreps.

"Shut up, Schuyler." Darthea yanked her gloves on.

"You shouldn't make her stay and you know it. You know
how they construct these buildings."

She scanned the walls, looking for the first crack.

"Jesus! Look at this!"

The yell came from the office two doors away from
Kreps's.

Darthea and I ran in. The skinny black-haired guy who was usually talking into his Dictaphone had spun his chair to his window. A newspaper blew in a whirlpool of air just outside.

"Twenty-eight stories up," he said. "I never saw that before. There's trash blowing around twenty-eight stories up! Bugs don't even fly up here!"

I leaned over the radiator and looked down. The entrance ramps to the Pike and the Pike itself were clogged with cars, a dead red stream of brake lights as far as the eye could see.

Schuyler Kreps smiled in the doorway, sucking the flame up his pipe.

"What a bunch of wusses," he said. "The snow will stop by six; it'll take them an hour to clear the roads, we can sit it out and be home free by eight."

A potato chip bag joined the newspaper, and they bobbed up and down jerkily, like a couple square dancing.

"I don't know," the guy with the Dictaphone said, mesmerized by the sight. "Like I said, I never saw anything like this before."

"'Bye everybody." Darthea broke into a trot and headed toward the lobby.

A phone call came through for me. Tia, the dog sitter, with *Gilligan's Island* playing on a TV in the background.

"Great," I said. "I'm so glad you called. I was getting worried about Lucas and the storm. Have you—"

"Sorry," she said. "My boyfriend and I had a huge fight this morning and I moved out, so I can't—"

"Moved out? To where?"

"I'm at my sister's. In Dublin."

"Dublin!"

"Dublin, New Hampshire," she said. "Look. I'm sorry. I just had to leave. You know how it is."

"Really, I don't. We had an agreement. My dog is sitting in my apartment, waiting—"

She hung up.

I called Jack and got his mother.

"No, my dear," she said. "Jack can't possibly drive to Cambridge. He's gone to Nine Acre Corner for food for the dogs. In seventy-eight we nearly ran out."

I moved into manic typing gear.

Shift indent the poor sucker's address. Enter Enter the office number. Enter Enter, print.

Make a little game of it. Make a mantra. I'll get to Lucas. I'll make it up to him.

"Hello!"

Was I imagining things? It was a woman's voice—a loud whisper. I stopped typing.

"Hello, Libby!"

It was Teresa, standing in the doorway to Darthea's darkened office.

I walked toward her.

"Teresa! What in the world are you—"

"Shhh—" she said. "Come in here. Don't turn on the light!"

Her hair and face shone with snow; she was wearing a parka that was too light for the weather and thin gray athletic socks for mittens. She was shivering.

"God, Teresa—you're going to get sick. What did you come in for? Did you think the cleaning company would fire you? I'll get some paper towels so you can dry off."

She grabbed my arm as I turned to go out the door.

"No!" she said. "I just want to give you something. Remember? What I told you about? Last week?"

"Sure, Teresa, but you didn't have to—"

She pulled an envelope out of the front of her jacket and shoved it into my hand.

"Here," she said. "Don't let them see it."

The envelope was large, brown, business letter size—the

kind you hardly see anymore. The address was handwritten in small, precise script with a fountain pen.

Andrea Hale
c/o Teresa Reyes

—at a street number in Charlestown. I couldn't make out the postmark; the light was too dim.

Teresa stepped farther into the corner of the office.

"It came to me," she said, "the week after she died. She asked me for a favor to let it come to me. I don't know why. I should have given it to the police, I know. Almost I—I mean I almost did one time. But—"

Her eyes were enormous with guilt.

"But I was afraid. Afraid that the police would ask me questions. I almost mailed it to them, but I was afraid that they would find my fingerprints."

"Afraid that they would tell the INS about you? That the INS would send you back?"

She nodded.

"And—"

"And what? Were you afraid of what might be inside?"

"I hate to be afraid. It's what I write in letters to my mother to tell my little girl: don't be afraid. But I was afraid."

I started to tear the envelope open.

"Don't!" she said. "Not here! Hide it!"

She gestured toward the front of her jacket. "Hide it like I did. Open it in your home."

I shoved the envelope into the front of my sweater to calm her down.

"Stay here for the storm, Teresa. You can sit in this office. Darthea won't be back. Somebody's got pizzas, and there's a Coke machine. You can—"

"No," she said. She tugged at the sleeves to her parka. All

the coolness and poise that she'd shown when we'd had our smoke-in three days before had evaporated. Her lower lip trembled; her shoulders sagged; she wouldn't look at me.

"I'm sorry," I said.

She stared at the carpet.

"Sorry for what?"

"I'm sorry that—"

The skinny lawyer with the Dictaphone marched down the hallway, this time without the Dictaphone. Teresa stepped deeper into the office.

"—that you have to be afraid."

The envelope was postmarked the week Andrea was murdered, in Revere, Massachusetts. I held it under my desk and sliced it open.

"How's it going?"

It was Kreps, hollering from his office. Now that we had moved into informal snowstorm mode the lawyers seemed to feel free to yell from inside their offices. A lot of them had turned radios on; I could hear the semihysterical murmur of weatherpeople from every corner.

"Okay!" I called back.

"You can call me Sky!"

"Okay, Sky!"

"Keep moving it!"

The envelope contained three sheets of notebook paper— white, with wide blue lines—the kind we used in junior high.

The front page was a note to Andrea, handwritten in the fountain pen:

> Dear Andrea,
>
> I enclose my report to date. This is painstaking work, as you can see.
>
> Records from your first and second years at

Saint Mary's no longer exist. I haven't spoken
with any of your family's neighbors, per your
request, but do encourage this as a usually fruit-
ful route.

And Andrea, as I told you when we met, my job
would be a hell of a lot easier if you'd tell me
what I'm looking for.

Warmest regards,
Lou

The next two pages were a chronology of Andrea's life,
starting with her birth in Lynn, referenced to documents that
weren't enclosed, like the birth certificate.

It was boring reading. Andrea went to kindergarten in the
town she'd been born in, graduated from Cardinal McNamara
Elementary School, where she had never received any grade
but an A, and from Saint Claire's Junior High, where she won
prizes in spelling, arithmetic, and conduct, and from St. Mary's
High School, where she was class salutarian—I'll bet that
burned her up. Her records reflected no detentions, no disci-
plinary proceedings whatsoever. She won attendance awards
in elementary school and junior high, but was sent home once
as a high school senior for wearing her skirt too short. (Atta
girl, Andrea! I thought). She was selected as a delegate to Girls'
State, and received two hundred and fifty dollars from the
Lion's Club and a one-hundred-dollar Edna Wilton Scholarship
toward her tuition at Rochester Institute of Technology.

The family had lived consecutively at three houses in
Lynn—each larger than the last, if property taxes and street
names were any indication.

"How are we doing?"

"Great, Sky."

I stuffed the envelope into my bag and banged out more
notices.

146

"Almost done, Sky!"

Incredibly young-looking lawyers, most male, some female, started roaming the halls. I've lived in New York long enough to get nervous about free-floating gangs during disasters. I pulled my bag under my desk.

I tried Jack again. My phone was dead.

"Phones are dead!" I yelled out, starting to get in the party mood myself.

"No they're not," somebody yelled back. "Outgoing's dead; incoming's not. Lexis is dead!"

"Long live Lexis!" somebody yelled.

I sent my notices to the printer, which appeared to be alive.

"The light on the Prudential Building is totally spazzing!" somebody yelled.

I brought the notices to Kreps. His face was pale; his eyes were wild. He motioned me out of the room.

"Forget them!" he said.

He was yanking on his galoshes.

"My wife just called," he said. "The baby's got a fever of a hundred and three and she'll never get her to a doctor in this!"

He looked like he was going to cry.

"How are you going—"

"I'll leave the car. I can take the T to Alewife and walk from there."

"Is there anything—"

"Jesus Christ. Just leave me alone. Let me get out of here!"

His open boot buckles made a jangling sound all the way to the lobby.

I looked in the kitchen for plastic bags to weatherproof the stripper pictures and Andrea's dossier. No such luck.

The Ueland Room—the conference room I'd bandaged the

big man's finger in on Friday—was almost debauched. Guys who could have been triplets—matching horn-rimmed glasses, red suspenders, white shirts, and big bottoms—played cards at the table. A nearly matching woman—same glasses, white shirt, blue skirt, strand of pearls, but normal-size bottom—poured Almaden into coffee mugs.

"House white," she said as she handed me one. "They keep it in bookkeeping so we can have it if we work late Saturday nights."

"Thanks."

"I'm Eileen."

"Penny." The name was coming more easily. In fact, I was starting to like it: no canned-vegetable connotations. A Penny for your thoughts. Lucky Penny. A Penny saved . . .

A similar party was going on in the Darling Room behind the receptionist's pen, but the drapes were closed.

"Partners' party," the woman in the pearls said. "They get champagne."

"Yeah. Fred pours all the leftovers out of the bottles after the closing parties into one jug and plugs it up. Like Mum's Fifty-Seven Varieties."

"Shhhh." A guy in a gray suit, older than the others, wearing rimless glasses like Franklin Roosevelt's, was hunched over the television. He held up his hand to quiet everybody down.

"This is bad," he said. "They're closing the T."

"Closing the T!"

"Hartman says he's going to bill all night!"

"Bill all night!"

"How are we going to eat?"

"Shut up!"

"Listen!"

FDR looked mad. "Listen. This is bad. The Tobin Bridge

started to buckle. There are cars stuck on it. They can't get any trucks there to tow them off."

The room went dead; all eyes turned to the screen.

The weatherman looked terrified. The scarf that he'd wound around his head was encrusted with snow; he held on to a STOP sign to keep from blowing away.

"Stay where you are," he said. "The governor has ordered all vehicles except emergency vehicles off the road. As of right now the roads are closed to all vehicles except emergency vehicles."

Somebody handed him a piece of paper.

"Ten beachfront Scituate houses just fell to the force of the storm surge. Viewers, this is without a doubt the worst storm in New England history. This—"

The camera went cockeyed.

Two of the coffee mugs on the table started to shake across the mahogany. All eyes turned from the screen and watched them putter their way to the pizza box at the far end.

"I'm getting out of here!"

"You can't." It was the Dictaphone guy. "You'll be killed. Tom, Jim, Harry—I want you to go to the kitchen and fill every vessel you can find with tap water. When you run out go to the twenty-seventh floor and do the same in the kitchen there—"

The three stood up.

"Okay, Bartlett, good idea."

"Yeah, good—"

"Listen!"

This time it was Eileen. Her eyes and mouth were wide open.

The weatherman had gone into a bus shelter, but he still looked petrified. "Confirmation of the story reported fifteen minutes ago: emergency workers searching through rubble

149

for casualties at the site of the collapsed warehouse on Pier Twelve have confirmed the identity of one body as Mark LeClair, the man believed to have killed Boston Attorney Andrea Hale during his escape from Wessex Superior Court last year. LeClair's body was apparently plastered or cemented into the wall of—"

"What pier was that?"

"That means he didn't—"

"He still could have. Somebody could have killed him later on—"

Eileen turned to translate for me.

"She was a partner here. Everybody thinks this guy—her client—conned her into helping him escape in the middle of his trial and then he killed her. But this means somebody else might have—"

"Eileen. That's enough. We each have our own opinion as to the Hale matter. We also have a firm policy of not talking to outsiders about—"

"But Bartlett, she's *working* here . . . "

"She's a temporary employee, Eileen."

"I know, Bartlett, but . . . "

"Hey you guys, shut up! We're trying to listen—!"

The building heaved, the television made pinging sounds, a collective moan of shock and fear rose from the Darling and Ueland rooms—a loud, visceral spasm of sound like the sound people make on the crest of the Cyclone roller coaster on Coney Island.

There was a thudding sound—the building settling, maybe, after the first swell. The lawyers' moan was softer this time. The lights shuddered, revived, then went out.

"I'm getting out of here."

"No you're not."

"The system! I've got the whole Raynax deal in there!"

"No hard copy?"

"Nobody move."

"The building's steel-reinforced."

"Oh yeah?"

"I think it tipped."

"The furniture's still standing up."

"Maybe we should stay in the center."

"Fred's going to have a fit."

"Fred will be sole heir."

"The phones are completely dead."

"What happened to the backup generator?"

Figures moved from the partners' party room into ours.

"Everyone remain calm."

It was a voice like Barbara Walters's—a little lopsided, extremely commanding—coming from a woman who sat down in the chair at the head of the conference table.

"It is vital that we take a head count immediately. I need light."

One of the triplets pressed a button on his watch and lay his wrist on the table. It leaked a weak blue haze over the woman's legal pad and illuminated the lower part of her face as she bent over, the way the light from a crystal ball would.

"Bartlett," she said. "Jameson. Cuthbert. May. Who else was in the Darling Room? No one knows? Bartlett, search both floors for anyone else who may still be here and report to me."

Footsteps thudded down the hall; a panting figure stopped in the conference doorway.

"Who is it?"

"M-mm-mmm-Mrs. M-Minnick!"

"Yes. Who is it?"

"It's Mr. Dunne, M-mm-mmm-Mrs. Minnick! Charlie Dunne. He's—"

"No. Who are *you*?"

"J-jj-Jay Randolph, Mrs. Minnick."

"There's nothing to worry about, Jay. We are perfectly safe in the Darling and Ueland offices. In my time as an associate with the firm I spent many, many entire nights here. We have food, we have—"

Jay Randolph was jumping up and down.

"For heaven's sake, James, stop that at once!"

"But Mrs. Minnick! It's Mr. Dunne. He—he—he's—"

"Speak up, James!"

"He's dead!"

He shouted it loud.

The rest of the people in the room surged for the door.

"Halt!"

It was Minnick's voice. Everybody stopped.

"Jay, are you absolutely certain?"

The kid's voice was steadier now.

"He doesn't have a pulse and he's not breathing."

"Where is he?"

"In the vending machine room. He—"

A couple of guys ran out the door.

"He what?"

"He was trying to pry open the soda machine. He told me not to tell. And then his arm just shot out in the air and he started gasping and then—"

"Did you administer CPR?"

"I tried, Mrs. Minnick. I know how to do it. But he was already d-d-d—"

"Dead. I see."

The room broke into a buzz. "Triple bypass" somebody said. "Wasn't even supposed to carry—"

Eileen was sobbing. The building was growing cold. A couple of people had lit cigarettes.

"Bartlett," said Minnick. "Report this to the police at once."

"I will, Pamela," he said. "When the phones are working."

Someone brought a portable radio into the room. Music was playing.

"Turn it off except for weather reports," Pamela Minnick said. "We don't know how long we'll be in here. Save the batteries."

"Yeah," Eileen whispered to me. "She might want to eat them."

"Yes, Eileen?"

"Nothing, Pamela."

"I'm sure you can find something useful to occupy your time. The Dictaphones still work. I, for one, am going to work on the *Reed* brief."

19

"Can I stay with you?"

The building's backup generator produced a mist of muddy-colored light at the end of the hall, just enough to let me figure out that the person who went with the voice was Eileen. She wore her coat, boots, and winter hat, and she was stomping her feet like she was trying to get snow off them, except there wasn't any snow; she was trying to get warm.

"Sure. But it's as cold in here as it is out there, and this couch wasn't built for people who have legs."

I'd been shivering on the sofa in Andrea's old office for hours, not really sleeping, not really awake, looking out the window into the dark of the blizzard and trying to shake recurring images of Teresa, huddled in a doorway somewhere between here and Charlestown, and Lucas, dead on the kitchen floor, out of my mind. The Burberry raincoat lining I'd found in the lobby closet made a lousy blanket; it smelled like Chinese takeout, and the cold air came in through the armholes. I wound it around my feet and willed myself not to shiver.

"That's okay," she said. "We shouldn't sleep. Something might happen."

Like we might freeze to death.

I never pictured myself dying that way before. I always figured I'd go fast and hard: a head-on collision on a rainy road; hit by lightning while taking pictures at the Virginia Slims Tournament; a violent altercation with my landlord, maybe.

"I wonder," I said, "if Schuyler Kreps made it home."

"Sky? Probably. The T was still running when he left."

She sat down on the floor next to the sofa, her back against the wall.

"You can feel the building vibrate when you do this."

"Thanks, Eileen," I said. "I'll pass."

"It gives me the creeps in here, too," she said.

"What does?"

"Being here," she said. "It's Andrea Hale's old office. Remember—what everybody was talking about in the conference room? Andrea Hale—the one who was murdered? Didn't you read about her in the papers? Where do you live, anyway?"

I was too tense and tired to dream up an evasive but credible response; fortunately, Eileen was the kind of person who never gave you a chance to answer a question before she hurtled on.

"It was terrible," she said. "I still think about it every day."

"I heard about it," I said. "I—"

"Listen," she hissed.

A high-pitched sound, a whistle on the edge of a buzz, had started up somewhere in the building.

"I never heard that before," she said. "I'll bet the building's cracked and the wind's coming through. What do you think?"

155

She stuffed her hands into her armpits and flapped her elbows as though they were wings.

"I can't get warm," she said, "no matter what I do." I threw her half the pillows from the couch; she used them to insulate her back and rear end from the floor.

"Thanks," she said. "I want to stay over here. I can't stand being on my side of the building, with—"

Her voice clenched.

"Charlie Dunne?"

"Yeah," she said, "with Charlie."

Her voice dropped to a whisper.

"He's right next door to my office. And Pamela's on the other side, still dictating her fucking brief."

"The rest of them," she went on, "are back to partying in the conference room. They ate everything out of the vending machine already except for the gum. They're so stupid. They don't realize—"

The whistling buzz picked up. It was almost as though something was flying around the building.

"They don't realize that this is for real?"

"That's right," she said. "That this is for real. They're kids. They're the kind of guys that nothing bad has ever happened to, so they can't imagine—"

My stomach whined.

"Is there any pizza left?"

She snorted. "Are you kidding? It disappeared even before the power went out. The guys probably put it in their pockets. And Pamela's sitting on the stash of soda that Charlie was trying to steal. I guess she wants to watch us beg for it."

The same kind of power trick Octavia would play at *Americans*. Except Octavia would probably order the weakest among us sacrificed right off. I could hear her now: "Olivia! The heels on your shoes are worn! Lay your head down here!"

Eileen pulled something out of her coat.

"Look," she said. "Tums. Brand-new. I'm supposed to take them for the calcium."

She squinted at me, assessing my age.

"You too," she said.

She shook some into my hand.

And when we're done with the Tums, I thought, we go to work on the Maalox. There was that big supply in the kitchen, unless the guys had already swiped it. Then of course there was the jar of Advil in Lorna's desk drawer.

The whistling stopped, then started again, louder. Eileen thrummed her fingers against the front of the desk, then rose to her knees.

"What's that?" she asked.

A second sound—a drone superimposed on the whistle—started up.

"Who knows?"

"Sorry," she said again. "I'll leave you alone."

"That's okay. Time passes faster, I think, if you talk."

Somebody walked down the hall carrying a flashlight, swinging it into the offices.

"You gals all right?"

"Yes, Bartlett," Eileen said.

"A couple of windows blew out on twenty-two. I think you ought to move to the inside. Maybe bookkeeping."

"Thanks Bartlett."

He left; I rose to go.

Eileen tugged me back down.

"Don't do it," she said. "I can't stand the idea of sitting in a room all night with them. What if Pamela Minnick's in there dictating? I'd go crazy. We can sit in one of those secretary cubbies instead. Which one's yours?"

We dragged the pillows out and stuffed them into my cubicle. Eileen sank down.

"Not so bad," she said, "for a place to die in."

"You're not going to die."

That's for sure, I thought. She'll be the only survivor—kept alive on pure nervous energy.

But I'll die, I thought. And Teresa and Lucas, too. And it will be my fault. Why didn't I persuade Teresa to stay here? Why didn't I leave when everybody else did? Why didn't I tell Schuyler Kreps to shove it?

Bartlett walked the hall again but didn't notice us.

We watched him disappear.

"I used to like him," Eileen said.

"Used to?"

"I used to like this whole place."

"So what happened?"

"Some stuff. You know. Whatever."

"I don't. You know I don't work here. I'm just filling in. I'm nobody."

A metal file cabinet let out a loud *ping*, contracting with the cold, I guess. We waited for the sound to happen again, but it didn't.

"What was it you were saying, Eileen—about why you don't like it here so much anymore? 'Some stuff' happened?"

"I don't know—" she said.

She craned her neck out of the cubicle, making sure, I guess, that Bartlett was good and gone.

"Fuck him," she said. "Telling me who I can talk to. Besides," she went on, "what would it matter? Who would you know?"

I kept my mouth shut. She settled back down.

"Well," she said, "first of all, Andrea Hale got killed, which I'm not supposed to talk to anybody about, like you heard. And everybody acted so weird about it. 'Don't talk to the press. Don't talk to your friends.' You know, it's so *unseemly*

158

being associated with something so *unsavory*. That's what one of the partners called it when he was telling us to shut up. *Unsavory.* He even asked if the cops would wear coats and ties when they came in to look at Andrea's stuff, so the clients couldn't tell what was going on."

"Did they? Put on suits and ties, I mean?"

"Of course not. So he made them use the freight entrance. Nice, huh? And then, the day after she was murdered—before the memorial service even—there was this feeding frenzy for her cases. Pamela Minnick—she was just made head of litigation a little while before—sat at Andrea's desk and passed them out like she was Santa Claus or something."

"So who got them?"

"Who? I don't know exactly who. I got some crummy ones. You know, a corporate client's wife being brought up on shoplifting charges—the kind of thing we don't usually do but sometimes we have to."

"How did she decide who got what?"

She was quiet for a while.

"Well, the juiciest ones," she said, "she took for herself. Like the big software copyright case Andrea was getting ready to try—I did a lot of the depositions—and then the rest of it was just people coming in and brownnosing for the good stuff. They say Pamela was crying while she did it, but—"

"But what?"

"I don't believe it."

"Why?"

"Pamela's the one who told the police about the phone call."

"What phone call?"

"You really are from outer space. The phone call where Andrea was calling LeClair pet names on the phone. 'Gumby,' or whatever. The day before the trial started."

159

"Maybe she was talking to her husband."

"Her husband? No. The police looked at phone records. We have them, too. For billing—you know. And her husband—John—"

"Ja—" I stopped myself.

"Says he never talked to her that whole day on the phone. But there was a phone call from the jail. They've got records of that. And Pamela heard her. She says Andrea had her office door shut—there's a policy about that—nobody's allowed to keep their door shut all the way—"

"What for?"

"I don't know. So everybody looks accessible or something. Whatever. But sometimes you have to close it to get any work done. Anyway, Pamela wanted to talk to her, so she says she opened the door and Andrea was swung around toward the window on the phone and didn't know that she was there, and she was saying—well, I'm not exactly sure, the police never released it, but it's what everybody here says Pamela says she said—"

"What?"

"Something like: 'I love you, Gumby, but I'm not sure I'm ready for this.'"

Gumby, Pokey, I thought. Same diff.

"And then she saw Pamela, and she said good-bye and hung up. Pamela says she looked really upset, like she was crying. And that when she asked Andrea if anything was wrong she said no, she just had a cold."

"Did she?"

"I don't know. I guess not."

"Did they like her? The other lawyers here?"

She digested that for a while.

"Well," she said. "It's hard to say. Liking doesn't have a lot to do with it. She didn't ever talk to me much. Sometimes I thought maybe she was jealous. You know—that she didn't like the idea of younger ones coming up the ranks—"

Not likely, I thought. Andrea probably just couldn't stand Eileen's chatter.

"But she was a good lawyer. A really good lawyer. And she loved trials. She couldn't wait to try a case; she'd get depressed if they settled. She was pretty good-looking anyway, but when she was on trial she'd get—what do they say about brides?—*radiant*. She'd get radiant."

I can imagine, I almost said, but stifled myself in time. That was how Andrea used to get when she was into her work at school, too. Her skin glowed; her eyes got sparkly.

"There was talk about her being a judge," she said. "But she put it off—asked for a deferral or something. She would have been great."

"So why didn't she want it?"

"The money, probably," she said. "She was bringing in major money here."

I doubt it was the money. People change, but Andrea couldn't have changed that much in seventeen years. She didn't have kids to send to school. She wasn't looking for a big showplace in the burbs, fancy vacations, fur coats, that kind of thing—I knew that for certain.

Or did I? I wanted to pull the investigator's report out of my bag again, scour it this time. What if Andrea had done something once that she was afraid would come out during the nomination process? What if she had hired Lou to do a background check on her to make sure she'd buried whatever it was well enough? If he couldn't find it, then maybe nobody could. Or maybe that was what she thought.

"You have to be pretty clean, don't you, to be a judge?"

"Clean? You mean you never got picked up DWI? You never screwed around with your income tax? Yeah, pretty much, I guess. But Andrea Hale? Heck, she was a shoo-in. She was Mrs. Clean—until what happened to her. I mean she even gave the ethics lunch for the summer associates."

"So she worked a lot? Slept here sometimes? Like Pamela Minnick?"

She laughed.

"She probably did. No kidding. She prepared for trials like crazy—which is what you have to do, you know. A lot of these guys—not just here, either—they get a bunch of flunkies to work on the case for a couple of years and then they step in the week before it tries and think they can learn everything then. Sometimes it works, but sometimes it doesn't, and then the client gets screwed. Andrea knew everything. She never even had to use notes in court. Juries loved her; judges loved her. Darthea and I used to play hooky sometimes just to watch her."

Her voice had gone rapturous—like a kid talking about his favorite baseball player, or like me, maybe, talking about Helen Levitt.

"Did you watch her at the LeClair trial?"

"The LeClair trial? Hey, you've got a pretty good memory, don't you? The trial she disappeared from?"

"Yeah."

"No," she said. "The partners would have freaked. They didn't want anybody spending time on that case but Andrea, and they weren't real happy about that, either. It was too—"

"Unsavory?"

"That's right. Too unsavory. And no fee, of course."

"So what was she doing it for?"

"Everybody's supposed to do pro bono work. It's supposed to raise the public's estimation of the legal profession. And—oh yeah—provide help to people who can't afford it. That's what it says in the associates' handbook. But it doesn't get counted in your billable hours, of course, and billable hours are all anybody cares about. You know, it's okay if you do a little free work for your son's private school, but beyond that—"

"And I guess Andrea went beyond that."

"You better believe it. The firm's name was in the *Herald*, for crying out loud—associated with *criminal work*. And then this stuff about her falling in love with the guy—"

"Do you believe it?"

"Me? I try not to think about it."

"Come on, did she seem like the type who would do something like that?"

Bartlett came through again.

"Girl talk?" he said.

"Yeah, Bartlett," Eileen said. "Girl talk."

"Three feet of snow," he said. "More out in Weston."

He kept walking.

"Weston's where he lives."

"I see."

"He gave me a terrible review this fall. He said I worked too independently. The time before that he said I wasn't independent enough. How do you like that?"

She ate some more Tums.

"Thanks, no."

"God, Penny, sometimes I wish I was somebody like you. No ambition. No complications. Home by five-thirty."

"I'm not home now."

"Oh yeah," she said. "That's right."

"So you were saying," I said, "about Andrea Hale. About whether you thought she was the kind of person who would do something like that. Spring her client."

"That's right," she said.

She rearranged herself on the pillows.

"I don't know," she said. "It makes me think about me, you know. I got caught up with a bad guy once. No kidding. I was a kid, seventeen maybe. I was lonely. My skin was bad. All I did was study. And then I started dating this guy who did time at a—what do you call it—a juvenile detention center. For stealing cars. My parents went crazy. And you know—I liked it that they went crazy. And I liked him. I liked how he smelled. I liked how he moved. How cute his butt looked in his jeans and how tight his jeans were. I liked how he didn't pretend to be something different from what he was. There's something about bad boys, I guess, when you've been a good girl all your life—"

Why was I thinking about Dan Sikora?

He definitely would not be a turn-on in tight jeans.

She poured herself some more Tums, sat up straighter.

"Like I said," she said, her voice crisp again. "I don't know. I didn't really know her very well."

20

THE STORM SLOWED AS THE SUN BEGAN TO RISE. THE FLAKES thinned in the watery light, then disappeared altogether except for a few caught in the chronic updraft at the side of the building. They flew skyward, providing the illusion that somehow it was snowing *up* this morning, or maybe that the world had turned upside down during the night.

Eileen and I stood at the massive Ueland Room window, marveling at the stupefying white stillness of the landscape. It was impossible to distinguish between the Common, the sidewalks, and the streets—they all lay together in a coma of snow.

After a while portions of the picture came to life: a plow ran on the east side of the Common, clearing the way for a Boston Edison truck behind it. The truck unloaded workers next to a web of downed lines; the sight was oddly comforting.

The crew that had spent the night in bookkeeping traipsed out. The triplets, the buckles on their galoshes jangling, headed out the lobby door to the stairwell. Pamela Minnick stepped into the conference room, a Hefty garbage bag in one hand, a pair of scissors in the other. She was wearing the fur coat that she'd worn all night.

"The T's running," she said. "But they're calling for more snow by noon. Bartlett and I are hiking to the police station. We've got to tell them about Charlie. I need you to help me with this. I don't know what the damp will do to sable."

She slit the bottom of the bag with her scissors, then held the bag against her coat.

"Now," she said. "Make the armholes here and here."

Eileen snipped; I stared. Pamela pulled the bag over her head and pushed her arms through the holes. It should have been incredibly funny but I was too tired to laugh, and Pamela, her makeup dissolved, her hair cockeyed, suddenly looked so pale and worn that I wanted to hug her, Hefty and all.

Eileen found an abandoned athletic bag in the back of a closet. We each got an extra pair of socks; Eileen used the towel for a scarf. I stuffed the raincoat lining into my jacket, then jammed my camera in.

We started down the stairwell. Twenty-eight stories. The voices and footsteps of the triplets echoed up the shaft. Eileen kept ahead of me, and after a while we could hear Bartlett and Pamela above us.

Somewhere around the tenth floor Eileen turned to me. She was crying.

"What's wrong? Are you sick?"

She waited for me to catch up. "No," she said. "It's just that the only other time we did this—came down the steps—it was a fire drill. Andrea Hale was here and she helped Charlie Dunne because his knees hurt. Everybody else went ahead," she said, "but Andrea stayed with him every step. She held on to his arm."

"That was good of her."

"Yeah," she said. "But not of me."

She was hiccuping.

"I went ahead, too," she said.

The T made it to Harvard Square in less than an hour. The Huron Avenue bus was another question; as it turned the corner from Concord Avenue it slid off the road and jammed sideways into a seven-foot-high bank of snow. We all had to climb out the back.

"Lucas," I whispered to myself as I picked through the drifts, "I'll never leave you alone again, honest. Be okay. I'll buy you horse meat. I'll get you a heated pillow—"

I tried to calm myself, reason with myself the way I had all night: of course he's okay; he's got extra fat on him. Sled dogs stay out days in the snow, don't they?

By the time I got to Fayerweather Street I could have dropped dead into the snow. My legs were rubbery; the cold air felt thick around my face; my eyeballs felt like something you'd chill a drink with. After trudging through the drifts it felt strange to walk on level ground, the way it does when you take off skates.

Someone had shoveled the sidewalk, but not the path to the house.

I'll get to that later, I told myself as I waded through. First I've got to warm up. First—

The front door was open.

The neighbors must be home, I told myself. They must be back from—

But their mail was still piled inside the common entrance, their newspapers, too.

The door to Jack and Andrea's place was closed but unlocked.

I pushed it open.

"Lucas?"

He usually hears me coming and runs to the door. Back on Canal Street he starts getting excited when he hears the elevator start up.

"Lukey?"

The heating system was creaking; he hadn't—

"Here boy—come on . . . "

He wasn't in the living room, the kitchen, the spare room, the alcove, the bedroom.

I locked the front door and searched the rooms again.

My hands went numb; I couldn't breathe.

Jack, I said to myself. Maybe his mother told him I called and he came after all. Although why he wouldn't bother to lock up . . .

I checked the basement stairwell.

"Lukey—"

Nothing.

I called Jack, fumbling the number twice because my hands were still so cold.

It rang and rang and rang. Eleven, twelve—maybe, I thought, he's on his way to Lincoln now with Lucas. Maybe he went out the back door; that's why there aren't any footprints. God, I thought. If he heard that report about LeClair's body he must be freaked. It would bring everything back to him, and he didn't seem in such good shape as it—

"Yes?"

It was Jack's mother.

"Hello Mrs. Hale. It's Libby Kincaid."

My voice and brain were operating on two different levels.

"Do you—I mean, does Jack—"

My throat clamped up.

"Jack's trying to get the plow up," she said.

"Does he have Lucas?"

"Your retriever mix?"

My what?

"Yes, my retriever mix. Lucas."

"No, he does not," she said. "Didn't we speak about this yesterday?"

"Yes, but—"

"Jack barely made it back from Nine Acre Corner before the worst of the storm. In the future, you should make arrangements with someone closer to your home. It's not fair to your pet and it's not fair to—"

I hung up.

I called the ASPCA; they put me on hold to a Muzak recording of dogs barking to the tune of "Jingle Bells." I called every Cambridge vet in the phone directory, the police, and a place called Angell Memorial Animal Hospital. Nobody had a dog that looked like Lucas—and—as the lady at the hospital reminded me—with three legs he'd be easy to "identify."

"Identify." The word sent my heart into a skid.

Sheets, slabs, toe tags.

I had to pee. I went into the bathroom, caught sight of myself in the mirror—the raincoat lining oozing out from under my jacket hem; my dead all-nighter complexion; my wild, teary eyes—and started to shiver.

Easy, I said out loud, trying to force myself to relax. Maybe a neighbor has him. Maybe he got out somehow and a neighbor—they're big on dogs around here—brought him in. They'd recognize him by now; we've walked up and down the street enough times. Besides, he's got all those tags.

My teeth were chattering. I turned the tub faucet on, ran the water hot, and stripped. My toes were bluish from cold.

I stepped into the tub. The showerhead was adjusted too

high; I pushed it down and aimed the spray into my face. It was hot—too hot, maybe—but I still couldn't stop shaking.

I dried off, cleared a circle in the steamed-up mirror with my hand, and took a comb to my head.

A strand of hair wisped across my face.

I held the comb to the light. The hair was coarse, strawberry blondish, about five inches long—definitely not one of mine.

Maybe Claire used it, I thought, back home.

That's crazy—it's the comb I keep in my travel case.

Maybe—

Maybe what? I hadn't had anybody in the condo since I got here except Jack.

I looked at the hair again. It sure wasn't his hair.

Maybe Jack gave a lot of old girlfriends keys to the place. Maybe that's how he kept it clean.

I got dressed and tried the ASPCA again. More "Jingle Bells."

I lay on the mattress and planned my search. I'd go door to door, to see if anyone had seen him. I'd call the police. Then I'd put notices up on the utility poles.

When was the second storm supposed to begin?

I turned the radio on.

The Grateful Dead slammed into the room.

What the—?

I dragged the radio onto the bed; it was tuned five stations past the station I kept it on.

I turned it off.

There weren't any footprints on the front walk. Whoever had been here could still be here.

I eyed the closed closet door.

But there weren't any dog prints either. I would have noticed that. Whoever it was left in the night, or maybe yesterday. With Lucas.

170

Somebody blond.

I thought about the showerhead.

Somebody taller than me. Somebody into nostalgia rock.

I checked the closets, my bags and boxes.

Everything seemed to be there.

The fridge was a mess, but that was my fault.

Only one thing seemed to be gone: the half bag of Purina Chow that I'd left in the cupboard under the kitchen sink.

Somebody who liked dogs, a half a bag's worth, anyway.

21

THE PROMISED SECOND SNOW BEGAN—FINE AND FAST, WITHOUT any of the previous day's false starts or lyrical preludes. I yanked my boots on; I wanted to knock on doors, find out if anybody saw Lucas leave the house, if anybody heard anything, if—

The doorbell rang.

Maybe it's someone who knows something, I thought, somebody who saw me come back home. I ran to the door and opened it. A woman, vaguely familiar—the owner of one of the Huron Avenue stores maybe?—stood alone on the porch, the snow gathering fast in the ridges of the scarf wrapped around her head.

"Hello," she said. "I hope I'm not—"

She looked into the entrance at the open condo door, then back to me. She scrutinized my face, like a doctor looking for bad moles at your checkup.

"We met . . . " she said.

It was the woman who'd tried to help me the night of the prowler. The one who'd had the little dog, except now she didn't. She was even wearing the same fringed scarf. In the daylight I could make out the paisleys.

"I'm Gretchen," she said.

She looked up the stairs again.

"Are you alone?" she asked.

My bottom lip wobbled.

"I can't find my dog," I said.

She put her hand on my arm and I pulled back.

"I mean your husband," she said. "Or is he your boyfriend? Is he up there?"

"I don't have a husband," I told her, "and I don't have a boyfriend either." Not anymore, anyway. Did Gail Sheehy write about this in *Passages*? About the part of your life when everybody who ever meant anything to you disappears?

"I know about it," she said.

"What?" About Andrea? Dan Sikora? Lucas? What was she—some kind of door-to-door psychic?

"I heard him last night," she said.

"Lucas? Where was he?"

She had kind eyes. A kind voice. Under different circumstances I would have liked listening to her talk. Under these circumstances I wanted to throttle information out of her.

"Last evening," she said. "I was out for my walk. With Stubb while the snow was starting."

Oh yeah, Stubb.

"It was about seven," she said.

She looked into the entryway again. What did she want me to do? Invite her in?

"And when we got here," she said, "in front of your house, I heard the yelling."

173

She was silent for a while. Snowflakes gathered on her eyelashes, but she didn't seem to notice.

"I felt terrible for you," she said. "No one deserves . . . "

"But Lucas," I said. "My dog—"

"I went back to my house," she said, "and called the police. They said they'd come. Did they?"

"I don't know."

"Surely you—"

"Honest to God. I don't know."

She reached into her coat pocket and pulled out a scrap of paper.

"This is my number," she said. "And the shelter's. Call me if you need me."

She turned and started walking.

A plow thundered by on Huron Avenue. By the time the noise stopped, the woman was near the corner.

"Hey!" I yelled. "Wait a minute!"

She looked back.

"What?"

"Last night. Did you see Lucas?"

She looked at me blankly. Maybe she couldn't hear me. I hollered again, blasting each syllable.

"Did—you—see—my—dog?"

"No!" she yelled, the word ascending, trapped in a sac of steam. "No!"

22

"DO ME A FAVOR. DON'T CALL THE POLICE."

It was Jack.

"You probably left the place unlocked yourself," he said. "I do that kind of thing all the time. I get thinking about something else. And the outside door doesn't always catch."

I'd talked to everybody on the block who was home. The lady with the walker, the Nigerian law student who invited me to go Morris dancing with him tonight, the woman who brought her knitting to the door and used me to measure the sleeve on, three or four people who were shoveling their walks.

Nobody had seen anything, heard anything, or remembered a dog with three legs.

I wanted Jack to help me. I wanted him to pick through snowbanks and plaster posters on telephone poles. I wanted to put pictures on milk cartons, hold a press conference, who knows what?

"Listen, Lib," he said. "If you'd been through what I've been through with the cops you wouldn't want to have anything to do with them, either. It's only been in the last couple months they haven't been breathing down my neck. I've only just started being able to concentrate again, feel regular again. I can't have them snooping around here again. I couldn't take it, Lib."

"Somebody took his food, Jack. And used the shower and my comb and played the radio."

"Did you check the trash? Maybe Lucas finished the bag already and you forgot. Maybe—"

"Maybe, Jack, you ought to get over here. If you'd come and taken care of him yesterday, this wouldn't have—"

"Relax, Lib. Maybe you gave a copy of the key to someone. Some guy, maybe? A kid looking for a better grade on his essay about the Influence of Snapshot Photography on—"

"This isn't a time for jokes, Jack."

"You think I'm joking?"

There was a pause while I thought about hanging up.

"Look," he said, "Of course I'll help you find him. I'll be out there as soon as I—"

He was talking to somebody.

"It's Mom," he said when he got back on. "She has a bad cough. I'm going to see if I can get her over to Concord to her doctor. She gets worried. A friend of hers died from pneumonia last winter."

"Swell, Jack."

"No, honest," he said. "I'll be over to your place first thing. After I take care of—"

Jesus, I thought. How could Andrea have stood this guy for so long? Mother this, mother—

"Right, Jack. See you, buddy."

Maybe he was the one using the condo as a whamming center. He didn't exactly have a lot of entertaining space out there at Mom's. Maybe the pictures under the table were part of his warm-up routine.

The pictures.

The investigator's report.

The presents from Manny's Joke Shop.

I started to sweat.

Where was the bag?

I checked the front hall.

Boots, puddle of melted snow, the Burberry raincoat lining.

No bag.

I rewound the trip home from Darling and Ueland on the screen in my mind. I couldn't remember much about the subway. The bus either. But picking through the drifts—I remembered that. I'd climbed some using both hands. I didn't have a bag. Definitely no bag. My camera, yes, tucked down the front of my jacket, but no bag.

No dog. No bag.

Was it still in the cubicle?

I called Darling and Ueland.

"Marie LaCosta."

"Marie," I said, "this is Penny. The temp. The one working for Darthea Cox and Schuyler Kreps. I wondered if somebody could—"

"I can't talk now, Penny. I'm walking the space with building management. There are some leaks."

"Are you open?"

"Open? Of course we're open. When will you be in?"

I hadn't thought about that.

"I just got home."

Silence.

I needed the bag.

177

"Whenever the T gets me there."

"Good," she said. "Just a minute."

I held on.

"Someone called for you," she said. "A little while ago. A man."

"Who?"

"He didn't leave a name."

Could Jack have tried me there?

"Thanks."

"Listen," she said. "I don't care so much about these things, but Fred frowns on personal calls at the office. There's a pay phone if you want to make an outgoing call."

"Okay," I said.

"I'm telling you this, Penny, because I like you. And because I think there's a very good chance that Fred will want to have a serious conversation with you when he gets back."

A flock of butterflies rose in my stomach. Had she called the agency? Had the agency called her? Did I call myself Libby by mistake?

"We like your work, Penny. You show a lot of promise."

"Thanks, Marie. That means a lot."

I rifled my notebooks for a slide that I could use on a poster of Lucas.

I kept coming up with Dan.

Dan dragging a birdbath out of his truck. Dan sitting at the desk in his shop, cleaning up an old neon clock. Dan the only time he ever came to see me in New York, glowering in the kitchen doorway. What had I done to provoke that look? I couldn't remember.

Then Claire during a heat wave, when we bought inflatable kiddie swimming pools and sat in them on the roof of the building. And Max—was this really the only picture I had of him?—holding his hand up in front of his face the way he always seems to do in pictures, like somebody being hauled in for an arraignment.

Lucas in the bathtub—too dark. Lucas in a party hat. No—it was just his head. I needed more than that.

Finally, I had it: Lucas on the sofa at Claire's mother's house in Maine, his head resting on a brocade pillow, one ear perked up at the whine of my flash.

My hands shook while I dug the slide out of its plastic sleeve. I remembered the moment I'd taken it:

Claire's mother had some musician friends in for the weekend. We'd played cards, eaten ourselves into oblivion. Right after I took this picture I'd run with Lucas on the beach.

I folded a piece of paper around the slide and closed it with a piece of tape.

God, he loved it there, dragging driftwood out of the surf, rolling around in the sand, chasing Claire's mother's Maine coon cat.

I bit back the tears.

I shouldn't have yelled at him so much for that. Dogs always chase cats. It's their nature.

I couldn't imagine life without Lucas. Life without Dan, well, just barely. Life without Max? I'd already spent most of my life without Max—it didn't require imagining. But life without Lucas?

For a long moment I couldn't move.

Then I looked under the sink again for the sack of dog chow, then in the trash, like Jack suggested.

Of course it wasn't there.

23

THE BAG WASN'T IN MY CUBBY, EITHER. THERE WERE SIX DICTA-phone tapes in my in box, though. All were from Darthea, who apparently spent the night at home cuddled under a blanket with her briefcase.

I'd left the slide of Lucas at a photo-processing place near the T entrance for a rush printing job. I thought maybe things would be slow with the storm so I could slip out of the office and pick it up, maybe work on the poster at my desk. Fat chance. The office was at what they call "skeleton staff" at *Americans*, the phones ringing nonstop and not enough people to answer them. My mind was 99.9 percent occupied with Lucas; the remaining .1 percent might just, I thought, be sufficient to transfer incoming calls.

If Charlie Dunne's ignominious death the night before bothered anyone, you wouldn't know it. Maybe, I thought, Darling and Ueland always feels like a place where someone has just died. Hushed and dim, with an undercurrent of desperate tension.

Lorna was there but barely acknowledged me. Too busy. A lot of catching up to do what with leaving early for the storm.

I straightened up the wastebasket, the mat under the chair, the spilled container of paper clips—all casualties of Eileen's and my soiree in the dark the night before. The bag wasn't there. Not on the floor, not in the drawer. Not in the closet where I kept my jacket, or in Schuyler's office, either.

Darthea was reading the paper at her desk. She looked relaxed today. Her hair was in a ponytail and she had pants on, the better for trudging through drifts with. I scanned the room for the bag but didn't see it. Darthea looked up.

"How about a cup of coffee?" she asked.

Bless you, I thought. You're a human being after all. I was nearly tempted to tell her about Lucas.

"Sure. Thanks, Darthea. I like it black."

She stared at me, then snorted like a horse.

"I mean, Penny," she said, "I want *you* to get *me* a cup of coffee."

Of course. How could I have been so naive?

"Have you seen my bag, Darthea? Black parachute fabric, the zipper busted? I think I—"

"No," she said.

I fetched the coffee. The bag wasn't in the kitchen, either. Or in the Ueland Room.

Who knows what I did with it? It had been dark in the offices; I was tired and worried.

I turned my computer on and stared at the little pulsing light that glides around in the documents, marking where you are.

Easy there, I told myself. All I need to do is relax. After I'm relaxed I'll be able to retrace my steps.

I rolled my head around on my shoulders the way I

learned to do in the free introductory yoga class I took last year.

There, I thought, that's better. That's—

A sound like a machine gun went off in the next cubby; the one nobody was ever in.

I leapt out of my seat.

"Jesus! What was that!"

Lorna leaned out of her chair.

"Compulaw," she said. "You never worked in a law firm before?"

I looked in the cubby. The only things on the desk were a CRT and a printer—the old-fashioned, prelaser kind that made a racket. Like the ones the photo department still has at *Americans*.

The machine was silent, then blitzed again.

"Don't bother with it," Lorna said. "It's probably just an ad. They're probably trying to talk us into adding a new service."

A couple or three sheets of paper, connected at perforations, rolled out of the machine.

I reached to tear them off but the machine fired another round.

"Honest." Lorna was exasperated. "It's just spilling out junk. Nobody uses Compulaw anymore. Now it's just Lexis. The lawyers and paralegals can access the system through their own terminals now and they print out at the printing centers."

I tore the paper off and took a look.

"Search update" it said at the top. "Lawyer: ASH."

"Okay," I said over the cubicle wall. "I'll get rid of it!"

Search saved: Huntoon w/15 construct! or plaster! or build!

Scope: global newspapers, periodicals

Update: 0 after previous six-month update.

Save update: Y or N

* * *

The rest was what Lorna told me it would be: exhortations to try the system's new Expert Witness search service, commercial journal search, things like that.

I switched the terminal on and saved the update. Did Andrea work for Huntoon, too? Had he been her client first, passed on to Schuyler Kreps when Andrea died? I opened the notebook that contained old time sheets. They only went back six months.

"You okay?" said Lorna.

"I'm okay. But Lorna—"

"What?"

"Did Andrea Hale ever work for Huntoon, that client of Schuyler Kreps's?"

She shook her head no. "Not a chance," she said. Then she lowered her voice. "She was too big of a snob. She wouldn't have gone near a guy like that. He's Schuyler Kreps's very own."

I pressed the first of Darthea's tapes into the Dictaphone tape player and put the headset on. The phone rang.

"Schuyler Kreps's office."

"Miss Kincaid?"

It was a woman.

"This is Mrs. LaCosta."

Marie. Why the sudden formality?

"Come to my office immediately."

This was beyond formality. The words sounded like they were dropping out of an ice machine.

"Sure," I said. "Where is it?"

"Next to the mailroom, Miss Kincaid."

Somehow I didn't think she was going to offer me that permanent job.

I walked down the hall, stifling a flashback to seventh

grade when I was sent to the principal's office for correcting my teacher's pronunciation of the word *library*.

"Come in and close the door."

Marie LaCosta sat at her desk, her arms folded across her chest. A man I'd never seen before, about fifty, bald-headed, in an undertaker suit, his legs crossed at the ankles, sat in a chair that he'd dragged to her side.

On one side of the desk there was a Rolodex. On the other side there was a calculator. In the middle there was my bag.

"Close the door, Miss Kincaid," she said, "and sit down."

Oh man.

Marie spoke without looking at me.

"This," she said, gesturing toward the man with her elbow, "is Rowan Saltus, our managing partner."

I held out my hand for a shake. He stared; I pulled it back.

"Do you recognize this bag?" she said.

"Well sure I do. It's mine. I wondered what—"

Okay, I thought. Now I remember. I brought it into the kitchen the night before, just before they turned on the news in the conference room. I'd been looking for something to wrap the papers in to keep them dry when I went outside.

"One of the building management workers found it," she said, "and when he looked through it he discovered a Darling and Ueland interoffice envelope. He brought the bag to me, and one of the girls identified it as yours."

"Thank you."

And thank you Lorna, I thought. Was this why she wasn't talking to me?

Rowan Saltus crossed his ankles the other way, then leaned forward just a little bit.

"Your private life is your own, Miss Kincaid," he said, not moving any facial muscles except the minimum it took to pull his lips around his teeth.

I lifted the bag from the desk. The bottom was wet—

184

soaked through. Saltus pulled the hanky from his pocket, dried the wood with it, and handed it to Marie.

"To be frank," he said, "we don't want to know any more than we do already. This was enough."

I looked inside the bag. The stuff from the joke shop was there: Claire's feather boa, the tassels, the trick gum. The pictures were there too, in the interoffice memo envelope I'd found them in, but the envelope with the letter in it that Teresa had given me was gone. I frisked the bottom of the bag to make sure, but the only thing left was an empty Pop-Tart envelope.

"More than enough," he said.

I put the bag in my lap.

"There was something else," I said.

"Excuse me?"

This from Marie.

"There was another envelope," I said. "Business-letter size. With some, uh, documents inside."

Rowan Saltus flicked his eyes toward Marie, then toward me.

"Was there, Marie?"

"If there was I'm sure I don't know about it," she said.

The bag was making a damp spot on my lap. I lifted it.

"Where did the man say he found this?"

Marie pressed some buttons on her phone.

"Ken—where's Al?"

A helicopter flew over the strip of the Charles River that I could see from Marie's window.

I wouldn't mind a bit, I thought, being in that chopper right now.

"Al," she said into the receiver. "Exactly where did you find that bag you brought into the office today?"

Marie hung up the receiver.

"He found it," she said, "at the bottom of the stairwell,

underneath the first flight of stairs. You must have dropped it on your way out of the building."

I knew I didn't have the bag then. I remembered having both hands free to clutch at the railing those last three or four flights of frozen stairs. I hadn't brought it down with me.

"I've called the agency," said Marie—

Oh boy, I thought, the feds are waiting for me out in the lobby.

"—and they're closed today because of the storm. So I've taken the liberty of terminating our relationship with you as of—"

She turned to Saltus.

"Now," he said.

"Now," she repeated.

"Please gather your belongings," she went on, "and leave the premises as quickly and as quietly as possible. The agency will take care of your pay."

The chopper was back, moving in the other direction.

"Okay," I said.

I can get those posters up tonight, I thought, if I work fast.

24

I STOOD IN THE CENTER OF THE ELEVATOR LOBBY WITH THE HANDLE
to my bag wound around my wrist. More than half of the elevators were still out of service. From snow getting in through
a crack in the roof, somebody walking by said. No, her com-
panion corrected her, because management's too busy working on the basement.

I thought about taking the stairs, then thought again; my
legs were still dazed from the previous night's trek.

Rowan Saltus walked by. Marched by, actually, marking up
a document in his hand, and disappeared into the reception
area.

I'd go straight to the photo place. I'd asked for rush service; maybe the print of Lucas would be ready.

The guy who joined me in the elevator on the tenth floor
looked me over.

"Why so glum?" he said, a big smile on his face. "You look like you lost your best friend."

"So what if I did?"

I walked through the narrow path that had been cleared on the sidewalk, between shoulder-high banks of snow, like a rat in a lab maze.

The fluorescent lights in the photo lab hurt my eyes after all the whiteness outside. I blinked and stamped the snow from my feet. The guy who'd written up my job—his head was shaved except for a pigtail growing out of the cleavage at the nape of his neck—was running a binding machine at the rear of the room. He ignored me while he finished the run, then looked up.

"Hey!" he yelled. "What's the matter with it?"

"What?"

"The print. The dog. I thought it looked pretty good. Considering how fast I did it."

"I haven't seen it yet."

"Nah," he said. "The guy you sent to pick it up said it was okay. Maybe you missed him."

"What guy?"

"You know, the guy. He—"

"No," I pulled the receipt from my pocket. "You've got it wrong. *I'm* the one who was picking it up. And here I am. Now."

A woman—the manager, maybe, she had hair all over her head—came over.

"What's the trouble?"

"A mix-up," I said. "He gave somebody else my job. I don't believe this. It was the best picture of my dog; it was—"

I started to choke on the words, then brought myself back.

"What did the guy look like? What did he say? Are you

sure it was my job he wanted? Did he write you a check?"

"How should I know? He said you sent him to pick it up. You were going out of town or something. Going to a meeting. He had cash."

The manager started looking through drawers.

"You gave him the slide, too? Did you get his phone number? Look on the check."

"Sure I gave him the slide. Why would I keep the slide? We don't keep slides. I was trying to help you out. He said you were in a big rush. It was still wet when he took it. Probably froze or something."

"He didn't have the receipt and you gave him the job?"

"What am I supposed to do? Give everybody who comes in here a lie detector test?"

The manager waved a stack of discount film-processing coupons in front of my face.

"Here," she said. "I'm sorry. Take these. Take all of them."

"What did he look like?"

"Like I said: I'm supposed to give them lie detector tests?"

"I said, 'what did the guy look like?'"

He shrugged his shoulders.

"How should I know? Big parka. Brown maybe. Black maybe. Scarf around his mouth."

He gestured toward the window. Two men in dark gray Chesterfield overcoats, scarves wound around their faces, fur hats on their heads, walked by.

"See—look at those guys out there. You think you can tell them apart? Figure out what they look like? It's cold out there, lady."

"Where did he go? What direction?"

"How should I know?"

"Honest," said the manager, waving the coupons again. "All these. For free."

* * *

Cars were moving—slowly, but moving—on Summer Street and down around South Station. I made my way to the garage I'd parked in the morning before the storm, walking in the street most of the time, trying not to slide into traffic, chewing myself out for being so cheap. I could have parked closer to the building, maybe at the Lafayette Hotel—that would have been clean and convenient, but no—

A tiny old man was throwing sand around on the entrance ramp to the garage. On one foot he wore a black rubber galosh like the guys at the firm wore; on the other he wore a built-up shoe. He crossed the ramp toward me, throwing the good foot ahead, dragging the bad one after it.

I couldn't find my ticket. It wasn't in my jacket pocket and wasn't in the zipper compartment of my bag, where I usually put things like that.

Good god, I thought. What's happening to me? I've always prided myself on traveling light, tight, and organized. Lucas. Lucas's picture. The envelope. My parking receipt. Where did they go?

"Hey," I said. "My ticket. I don't know what I did with it."

"What the hell," he said. "Give me sixty bucks."

"Sixty bucks? Are you kidding? I don't have any sixty bucks. There was a snowstorm. An act of God. You're supposed to show a little mercy. A little—"

"Okay," he said. "Twenty."

"Twenty."

I counted out two tens, then added a five.

"Sorry," I said, "for having a fit. The storm's got me on edge."

I started to walk to the entrance door by the ramp.

"Can't use it!" the guy screeched. "Lock's busted. Or froze. You gotta go around the side. See?"

He walked to the curb.

190

"That way," he said. "Around there and then the back. It was the only door I could get open. You're lucky you can get in at all. You shouldn't have left your car."

I followed his instructions, picking my way through drifts of snow, frozen garbage, frozen abandoned tires, and what looked like the back end of a frozen rat sticking out of a Burger King bag. I didn't want to know for sure. I finally made it to a scarred black enameled steel door propped open with a hubcap.

I opened it and crossed the concrete to a stairwell. The door was massive; the handle was loose. I thought at first that it was locked, but it wasn't; my arms were just weak from—what? The cold, maybe. From getting fired. From thinking about Lucas. I climbed the stairs.

My Rabbit sat alone in its row, in the shadow of a concrete pillar.

I felt a gush of near-love for her—the one constant in my life. So the exhaust system falls out once in a while. So the back doors don't open from the inside. She's there, isn't she?

The driver door unlocked like a dream.

"Good girl," I told her, and sat down.

"Attagirl, now just—"

I turned the key.

She whinnied.

Whinnied.

Whinnied and died.

Easy, I told myself. You don't want to flood her. The guy downstairs can give you a jump start. Just—

Whinny.

Whinny.

Kachink.

I got out and opened the trunk for the jumper cables.

I could feel them, but they were snagged on something as usual—the tire jack, maybe.

191

That's how I'll make my million, I thought. Jumper cables that retract onto a spool, like a measuring tape.

I freed part of the cable; then the metal clip broke off in my hand.

Damn. Claire was right. I should join AAA every year, the same time I pay my insurance premium. Maybe if I called and joined now—

"Need some help?"

I pulled my head out to see whose voice it was, but it didn't matter. He had my arms behind my back before I could make out anything but a shoulder of dark-color parka. I bit at it, getting nothing but a mouthful of polyester that slid out of my teeth. I started to scream, then felt the gun behind my ear.

I couldn't move.

For a moment I wondered if I'd been shot in the neck and paralyzed.

No. I just couldn't move.

A voice rang up the stairwell. Hollow, banging off the metal.

The scream was stuck in my throat like a chunk of ice, keeping me from breathing, from thinking, from moving.

"Everybody okay up there?"

It was the attendant, the old man.

My assailant hissed in my ear. Hot breath, cold gun. Bad aftershave, bad breath.

He had a scarf around his chin and mouth; an orange acrylic hat pulled low over his forehead. All I could make out was brown sideburn stubble on fatty, purplish skin, and his ear, which was ugly-looking. Too many folds in the lobe or too many lobes. Real ugly.

"Say something," he said, "and I'll blow your fucking eyes out."

Wasn't it supposed to be 'I'll blow your fucking *brains* out?'

Hai Karate. Aqua Velva, maybe. Something like I used to buy Max for Christmas when I was a kid.

Max, I thought. Please, no. I can't die and not have talked to Max.

The block in my throat grew bigger.

No eyes.

"Everything's okay," the guy yelled.

His voice was huge, magnified by the concrete, magnified by my fear. It was calm, smooth, confident. The voice of a man talking to the neighbor in the next driveway about a football game, the voice of a man calling up the basement stairs to his wife about what time lunch would be ready.

"I'm helping the young lady with her engine," he said. "We got the cables worked out. We're fine."

"Okay?"

"Okay."

The stairwell door clanged. Okay? What was with that guy—the attendant? What did he think we were standing like this for—me with my arms macramed behind my back, squeezed against a guy I didn't come into the garage with?

I remembered his leg, his awful limp.

He'd walked around the building on the ice, up the two flights of stairs to see if I was okay.

And then he left.

I wondered if he would have bothered coming out of the stairwell if I'd given him the sixty dollars.

The man's arms—one wrapped across my chest, the other pressing the gun to my neck—tightened. Now he dragged me across the floor.

I ground my heels into the concrete, laying a patch. I could hear Claire's voice, reading to me from the paper: "If they get you in the car, you're dead. Ninety-eight percent chance you're dead, it says. Ninety-eight percent."

His parka was slippery. If I wiggled, I thought, maybe I could slide out and roll under a car. But I couldn't budge. If I budged my arms would break.

His car was salty, filthy; the trunk was already open.

Here we go.

He bent to grab me behind the knees.

Ninety-eight percent, I thought.

I wrenched my right arm partly free and jabbed him with my elbow. It sunk into a couple inches of down jacket; I could feel the air puff back into my face.

My eyes, I thought.

He cracked me on the skull with the gun.

25

I was swimming. Floating, more like it. Dead man's float.

No gravity here. No up, no down. Just rocking, swaying, tipping, floating.

The jellyfish.

You grab your ankles and bob, facedown, the weight of your head pulling you forward, the weight of your rear end pulling you back. Tip forward, then back. Forward, back. It's summer and it's nice and don't worry, the water's not over your head, just up to here. Look—you're swimming!

But I wasn't.

I was in a car trunk, my left cheek in a puddle of vomit, my shoulders wedged bottom to top.

I barfed again, and the new barf pooled beneath my cheek.

At least, I thought, *I can tell which way is up.*

How long had I been out?

No way of knowing.

195

I twisted myself away from the stink the best I could.

Can't do that again, I told myself. *You could choke. Kill yourself.*

We were stuck somewhere. Not really stuck—moving slowly. On an entrance ramp to the Pike, maybe. Getting on the expressway, maybe.

The car lurched forward. My Leica, stuffed inside my jacket, dug into my chest.

Probably cracked the lens, I thought. *Smashed the viewfinder.*

Roll back.

Damn!

The goose egg on the back of my head pressed into the inside lip of the trunk opening.

Forward.

Back.

The guy had a heavy foot.

I was lost in a sea of fumes and engines and horns.

Blow your fucking *eyes* out, he'd said.

I can't see, I thought.

Maybe he did—

Of course it's dark; you're locked in a car trunk. Detached retinas, maybe—

It's because there's no—

Your fucking *eyes,* he'd said.

I screamed. A long, hysterical, roller-coaster ride of a scream, louder, longer than I knew I could scream. A scream that started in some black pit in my unconscious—fueled by every fear I ever had—of snakes and strangers and basements, thunder, darkness, death. And when it ran out I did it again, and again, and again, until I was empty.

Empty and weirdly calm.

There, I thought. Claire paid three hundred dollars to do that with a doctor. I got it for—

A new sound thrummed through the trunk. I could feel the vibrations in my shoulder.

I pressed my ear harder against the floor.

He was playing the radio. Loud. As loud as it could go. And he probably had the window open.

Save your breath, I told myself.

How much air could there be in here, anyway?

I could try to pry the partition between the trunk and the backseat away, but where would that get me? Sitting in the car with this guy? What did I expect him to do? Apologize and take me to Pizza Hut?

I heard Claire's voice again: Ninety-eight percent, Lib. Ninety-eight percent.

I tried to figure out a way to pivot to my back; that way I could mess with the lock. If I could latch my toes onto something, then throw my hips around to the right—

My boots were thick. Too thick and clumsy. But the rubber bottoms were good; they gave me some friction. The trunk was shallower at the sides than at the center. I wedged both feet heel to toe from the trunk bottom to the top and used the leverage to haul the rest of my body around so that I was lying on my back.

I panted with the effort, felt the blood pulsing fast through the tender spot on my head.

We were on smooth highway now, doing maybe fifty-five, sixty. Sand or gravel or whatever it was they use on the roads here gushed against the bottom of the car; the radio's bass still thumped through the partition between the trunk and the backseat.

I tried to slow my breathing, count my blessings. I wasn't tied up. I wasn't bleeding much. I was cold, but I wasn't freezing; I was benefiting from the warm air in the passenger compartment. Now if he stopped the car, left me in it, that would be a different story.

I pulled my gloves off with my teeth and stuffed them under my right shoulder so I'd know where they were. Ready for business, I told myself. You can do it.

The music stopped, eclipsed by the sound of the man's voice. He was yelling, but I couldn't make out the words.

The car was still moving.

Maybe there was somebody else in there with him. I hadn't thought of that.

The car swerved to the right, stopped, backed up, stopped again.

This is it, I thought. He's leaving me here. He was talking to somebody on the car phone who's picking him up, and he's leaving me here.

He's leaving me here or he's getting ready to take me out.

That would be faster, anyway. Faster than freezing to death.

The car lurched again, and we were back on the highway. Back to the whir of tires, salt, the banging radio bass.

A three-point turn. That's what he'd done—a three-point turn. He forgot something?

I writhed to my right side.

My teeth were chattering.

Easy, girl.

The lock was where it should be, covered by a smooth square of metal about the size of a cigarette pack.

How thoughtful. These car manufacturers think of everything: the kidnap victim needn't even worry about snagging her nylons.

I ran my fingers over the shield, but they were too cold and thick-feeling to make out any details.

I pulled them into a fist and slammed it against the metal.

I curled into a ball, pulled my face in front of the lock shield, and licked it with the end of my tongue.

No seams. No screw heads even.

No place to—

Hey—now we had something!

It was a hole, a square hole in the panel.

I pressed my tongue farther in and felt a tiny curved piece of metal, clearly part of the lock apparatus.

I blew against my fingertips and my knuckles, trying to warm sensation back into them, then touched my ears. I was still wearing my real faux pearl earrings—the ones I thought made me fit right in at the firm.

You can do it, I told myself. Think of Houdini. Think of Little Jessica who fell in the well. Think of people who get buried and— No, don't.

I pinched the back off one earring, then transferred the front—the pearl with the post—from my left to my right hand, slowly, carefully, like someone doing microsurgery. I felt for the hole in the lock shield again and pressed the post into it.

The earring slipped off the metal bar, but I didn't lose it.

I lined it up again, this time dead center, absolutely perpendicular—

The car stopped and threw me on my shoulder, then forward. The back of my head felt like somebody had driven a meat thermometer into it. I raised my hands in a reflex to protect my skull.

The earring was gone.

Shit, I hissed.

This is it.

A geometric pattern—prismatic triangles in red and purple—spiraled across the backs of my eyelids.

The pattern stopped and then I saw the stubble on the guy's cheek again. Black stubble on fatty, purple-pink skin. And the ear. Splayed, fringed, like a rose of flesh. A cauliflower.

A cauliflower.

This time I heard Max's voice.

"Cauliflower ear, hun. Bet you never saw one of them before. Look at it, bunny. Don't be scared."

We'd been at the service station in Darby where Max used to hang out. I must have been real little if he was still living with us.

The man's ear was awful. A glance was enough. I drove my face into Max's leg.

"It's just from boxing, bunny. Ain't it funny? Cauliflower ear."

I could see the men's trousers—dark green, dark blue, grease-stained—and hear them laughing. Maybe at Max, maybe at me. Maybe at the guy with the ear.

I never could eat cauliflower after that.

Boxing.

I could see the receptionist at Darling and Ueland batting her eyelashes, patting her hair, watching Huntoon through the conference room window.

"Used to be a boxer," she said. "And he still looks nice. And honey, he's loaded. He's got the biggest construction company in—"

In where?

Massachusetts, maybe?

The world?

I wormed my way to my right side and went to work on the other earring.

We turned sharp to the right, then to the right again. I held on tight to the earring, afraid I'd lose that one too.

We were on a rutted road. I couldn't hear any other cars around us. No horns, no engines, no hypnotic spray of gravel and sand.

Out in a field, I thought. Out in the middle of some nature preserve nobody goes to in the winter. In some toxic waste site in New Hampshire nobody will dare go near. By a lake that hasn't frozen over. By a—

We turned again, went real slow, and stopped, tilted, like the car was up against a curb or a bank of snow.

The engine died; the car door slammed.

Footsteps moved around the trunk, then faded.

Then everything was quiet.

My hands shook. I brought the earring to the hole in the panel.

And then I heard—

Lucas.

Absolutely. I know his bark the way they say blindfolded mothers can pick out their newborns in a nursery just from the cry.

Then I started to cry, the tears running down my temples and into my hair.

Lucas.

Far away.

Scared. Sensing trouble. Barking the way he barks when I'm walking him at night on Canal Street and he sees a weirdo in the alley. The way he does when somebody gets on the freight elevator in the middle of the night.

I inhaled, then pressed the earring post into the hole while I exhaled—the same thing I do when I press the shutter on my camera. Steadies the hands, distracts the nerves. Something like that.

Don't worry, baby, I whispered. I'm coming.

The latch made a beautiful crunching sound, a spring or hinge twanged, and the trunk lid sprang open.

Cold, fresh, tree-scented air rushed in.

I drank it like water, then hoisted myself out, shielding my eyes from the light.

My driver was gone. I pressed the trunk lid shut behind me

as quietly as I could, then crouched behind the left rear fender, where no one could see me from the house, I hoped. The change in position and the exertion brought new blood to the bump on the back of my head, made the row of bushes to the left of me undulate against the snow.

Steady, I told myself.

I focused on the metal letters bolted to the car— S-K-Y-L-A-R-K—encrusted with salt.

Don't forget to breathe.

We were in the suburbs somewhere. Not Lincoln-Concord suburbs. Different suburbs. Suburbs with ten- or twenty-year-old houses that looked like Tara in "Gone with the Wind" except they had three- and four-car garages. Suburbs where people had street numbers attached to their mailboxes, basketball hoops instead of tennis courts, snowmobiles instead of horses.

He had parked at one foot of a circular driveway, almost in the road. So the neighbors couldn't hear me scream, I figured.

The house at the keystone of the drive was massive and slanted on its lot, with an igloo-size boulder in the terraced garden next to the front steps. Sort of Colonial, sort of Victorian, sort of contemporary. The kind of place realtors advertise in the paper as "Executive Living": four or five bathrooms, central air-conditioning, no reading lights.

The house's front door was slightly open. The sun glared off the oblong panes of glass inset on either side of the door knocker.

I scanned the neighborhood. I could bolt; maybe call the cops from someone's phone.

The house to the left was under construction; newspapers were piled in the driveway of the house to the right. The house across the street—

Lucas barked again. A kind of garbled shriek, the kind he

202

makes when I step on his tail by mistake. He was in the house, no doubt about it.

I ran up the drive, up the steps, and through the door.

I was standing on a polished pink granite floor in an alcove that led to a circular entrance hall. A curved staircase ran to the second floor, a satellite-style chandelier swung from a gold-tone chain that hung in decorative loops across the ceiling. Something rank, liquid potpourri, maybe, in a winter scent—bayberry? pine?—filled the air. "Swanky," my ex-stepmother, Iris, would say.

To my right was a vestibule with hooks for coats, plastic trays for boots, an umbrella stand. I took off my boots so they wouldn't squeak on the granite and set them next to what looked like a pair of metal leg braces. One slid toward me; I caught it before it crashed to the floor. No, it wasn't a leg brace, but what was it? It was a foot and half high, maybe, with something that looked like a stirrup about fourteen inches up. Paint—no, plaster, had dried in drizzles down the sides.

Plastering stilts. I'd seen somebody in these once, when they were redoing the library ceiling at *Americans*.

One had a rubber tip at the bottom; the other didn't. I knew where it was. In my jeans pocket. Somebody used these plastering stilts to look in the bedroom window at the condo. That accounted for the scraping sound.

I stepped back out to the entry, skating a little on the granite with my socks.

To the left was a set of French doors. I looked through them into a formal living room: peach-color carpet, a fireplace rigged with glass doors, uncomfortable-looking sofas, a tremendous oil portrait of—

Andrea.

Could it really be?

My heart felt like it had torn from its moorings.

I couldn't hear anybody, couldn't see anybody.

I opened the French doors and stepped into the room.

Andrea. At what? Sweet sixteen?

It was kind of hokey-looking. Like somebody had painted it from a mailed-in photograph. Renoir meets Hallmark. Andrea on a scroll-back chair, wearing a pink taffeta dress with puffed sleeves, add-a-pearl necklace at her throat, ankles crossed, her hair a foam of curls at her shoulders, her expression all sweetness, all compliance.

There was a fancy signature in the corner of the canvas. *Elena diEilena.* And a date.

Two years ago.

I didn't get it.

Maybe I was reading it wrong. Maybe—

Something crashed upstairs. The ashtray on the table at my knee leapt and shook, the French doors jangled. I gasped, then covered my mouth.

Why wasn't Lucas barking?

Where was he?

I stood still, waiting for a response to the crash, but there wasn't one.

A door at the back of the room led to a hall, then to a kitchen. Big, with shiny floors, pots hanging from the ceiling, a butcher-block island in the center with an extra sink in it, the smell of Lysol or Mr. Clean.

The counters seemed low, or maybe I seemed high. Oxygen deprivation from being in the trunk maybe.

I padded, absolutely quiet, across the floor to the island, listened for sounds from upstairs, and pulled open the drawer beneath the cutting surface.

Perfect. It was like the display counter at the Hoffritz in Grand Central. Cleaver, bread knife, carving knives, paring knives. I picked out the shiniest carving knife.

There was a phone on a small desk beneath a shelf of recipe books. I picked up the receiver, my fingers prickling to dial 911, but there was no dial tone. A phone was off the hook somewhere else in the house. I remembered the crash upstairs; maybe, I thought, whatever turned over took the phone with it. I listened for a moment, but heard nothing.

I started to hang up the receiver, then froze. The notepad next to the phone had the same kind of paper in it that Andrea had written her poem on. The girl walking on the beach, the footprints . . .

The refrigerator motor kicked on. I shuddered, aimed the knife point down—the way they teach you to walk with scissors in grade school—and moved to a shallow downward flight of stairs at the far side of the room. A ramp ran along next to them.

They led to another big room. The entertainment center, I figured they would call it. Man-size, with man-size plaid sofas, an electric organ, a big-screen projection TV, a minirefrigerator next to a reclining chair.

Glass cabinets filled with trophies, photographs, autographed baseballs on little pedestals, weird-looking ceramic sculptures of baseball players with gigantic heads, ran the length of the room.

The cabinet nearest to me had a silver loving cup in it. *Mary Marlene Frank*, it said on the base, *First Runner-Up, Miss Commonwealth of Massachusetts*. Next to it was a framed photograph of a woman in an early sixties beauty-pageant getup: V-necked tank suit, traffic cone breasts, pretty face obscured by thick eye makeup, a hairdo big enough for a squirrel to live in.

The center cabinet contained just one thing: a leather belt, about three inches wide, with a brass doorknocker-like medallion in the center of it. *Gustav "Rocket" Huntoon*, it

205

said. U.S. Middleweight Champion, 1958. It reminded me of an electric male potency belt I saw in a 1916 Sears catalog once, with lightning bolts drawn around it.

I put the knife in my left hand and opened the cabinet. Then I reached in with my right and lifted the belt out, careful not to thunk the medallion on the shelving, careful not to—

There was another crash upstairs.

"Daddy!"

The shriek came from the front of the house. The living room, maybe, the front hall—

Lucas moaned. A contorted, muffled moan.

I ran through the kitchen, through the living room, opened the French doors to the entry, and looked up.

Gus Huntoon, the man I'd put the Band-Aid on in the conference room, stood at the top of the staircase, his back to the railing.

"I should've done that a long time ago! We were too soft on you! I told your mother we were too soft!"

A door opened at the top of the stairs and a teenaged boy, no, a girl—her neck was too thin to be a boy's—her head shaved except for a lacquered blond ridge that ran Mohawk-style down the center—peered out. I couldn't make out her face; half of it was covered with a towel. She was whimpering.

No, she wasn't whimpering. Lucas was whimpering. He stood behind her in the doorway, trying to push his snout between her leg and the door.

"Who do you think you are—lying to me! Your father! Dragging me out here under false prefixes! Shaving half your hair off! Lying about your mother! Where is she? What did you mean calling me in the car and telling me she was sick so I'd come rushing home? What kind of sick, perverted liar are you, anyway?"

The guy was out of breath; his shoulders heaved while he held the railing to steady himself.

"Get out of that bathroom," he yelled. "You want to fight? I'll fight. I'll show you who's—"

Where was his gun?

He let go of the railing, then straightened himself up, ready for another round.

"I've had it, Stephanie," he said. "You've been pushing me. And you've been pushing your mother, too. You know it's not good for her, Stephanie. You're killing her. You're killing your mother. She dies, girl, and it's your fault. You could've thought of her, Stephanie, before you went and found that woman. Why didn't you think of somebody else besides your own goddam self for once? You think the world revolves around you, don't you? Well I got news for you. I got—"

Lucas's eyes locked on mine.

Down, boy, I willed him. *Keep still another minute. I've got to think. I've got to—*

It was no use. Lucas shot out of the bathroom like a cannonball, spun past Huntoon, and skidded down the stairs at me.

Huntoon straightened, roared, and pulled his gun from his pocket.

"Daddy, no! Stop it!"

"Stay, Lucas," I told him. "Stay right here."

Huntoon walked down the stairs, slowly, his legs stiff and far apart.

What was that affliction? Cauliflower knees?

I held the middleweight belt in the air in front of me with my left hand and touched the knife to it with my right.

"Drop the gun, Rocket," I said.

He kept walking.

"The fuck I—"

"Drop it."

He was at the bottom of the stairs, ten feet away from me.

The belt leather was old, soft, starting to rot. The knife point went through it like a hot blade through butter.

Huntoon's face screwed up like somebody just messed with his private parts.

Lucas, I realized later, sensed Huntoon's window of weakness—his pain, his lapse of focus.

He soared across the entry in one fluid arc of three-legged muscle and fur, taking Huntoon down in a spasm of shock and wails.

The gun clanked to the floor, still within Huntoon's reach.

"Get him off me!" Huntoon was on his stomach. Lucas's jaws were wrapped around his upper thigh. The man pushed at Lucas's head with his hands, sobbed, kicked his feet.

"Get him off! He's killing me! Steffie, get the gun. Steffie— do what I tell you! Tell her to—"

Steffie was frozen halfway down the stairs, one hand still pressing the towel to her face, the other held palm out, as if the gesture could ward off the blood, the gun, the truth. I grabbed the gun and trained it on Huntoon.

"He's killing me!"

"Stephanie," I said, "it's time for you to call the police."

"Don't, baby—" Huntoon yelled. "If you love your old man you won't—"

Stephanie turned and disappeared into a bedroom.

The harder Huntoon pushed against Lucas's head the harder Lucas held on.

Chinese finger-trap, I thought.

Good.

I kept my eyes on Huntoon, but in the nimbus of my field of vision I saw Stephanie reappear. She dropped the towel, descended the staircase, and stopped on the landing, directly across from me.

Except for the swollen crescent of bruised skin that ran

from the corner of her mouth to her right temple, the radical hair, and the silver ring that encircled the bit of flared flesh at the rim of her nostril, she was Andrea twenty years ago. The same broad nose, the same squared brow, the same heavy-lidded eyes. She was the girl in the portrait, not Andrea. She'd done everything she could to conceal it, but she was the same girl. And her face was Andrea's: intelligent, focused, deep.

She stared at Huntoon, then at me.

"He was going to kill you," she said. "He's been following you around, just like he does me. He took the plate off my car yesterday, like he took the plate off the car he stole to get Andrea with. He followed me to Fayerweather Street last night, too. He was trying to figure out where you live."

She spoke calmly and distinctly, like someone delivering the commencement address at school.

Huntoon managed to writhe to one side, exposing a smear of blood on the pink granite. Lucas held on.

"He was going to kill you," she said, "just like he killed her. And that man, too," she went on. "The one in the—"

She sank to the bottom step, unable to keep her eyes off Lucas and Huntoon. Her voice collapsed to a whisper.

"—in the wall. The one who froze."

"You're talking about Andrea Hale? The lawyer?"

"Yes," she said. "Andrea Hale."

"He knew that you had been talking to her. That you'd found her. That you knew she was your mother, or thought so, anyway—"

"Yes."

"Because you'd seen her pictures in the paper—pictures from way before he killed her. Like when she won her big case. You knew that she looked just like you and you figured out that she was the right age to have had you when she was a teenager."

She nodded. "That's right," she said. "And once a man downtown, somebody who worked in a sandwich place, told me I looked like a lady who used to come in there for lunch. Once he even thought I was her for a minute. I went there every day for three weeks, but she never came."

"Did you ever get to see her? In person? To talk to her?"

Huntoon's eyes were closed.

"It was killing her mother," he said. His voice was a wheeze. "My wife."

The girl looked over him and at me. "My mother," she said, "my adoptive mother, has MS. You never know, but right now she's doing great. That's what counts. Right now. How she feels right now."

She picked up strength while she talked; the frightened edge was gone from her voice. She stood up, her eyes glowing. Now and again she raised one hand and made a twisting motion with it to emphasize a word. Just the way Andrea had.

"She's swimming right now at the Y," she said. "She has a van that's rigged for a wheelchair and she has a friend who meets her there. She's doing great. She's a fighter. She's a—"

"Don't tell her anything," Huntoon interrupted her. "You can't trust her. She's Jack Hale's girlfriend. They're in this together. I'm telling you, Steffie, what do you know?"

Stephanie circled him, stopping where she could look him in the eye while she talked.

"I can trust her, Dad," she said.

She leveled her gaze at me.

"I checked her out."

She sure did. Staring through my bedroom window with a flashlight to see if I was sleeping with him. Out there in the snow on those plastering stilts.

"You didn't have to be so scared, Dad. Mom knew what I was doing. She said she'd do the same thing if she were me.

But she was scared to talk to you about it. Scared of you, Dad. You know that. You've made a career out of scaring people. You're a professional."

He was the one who'd been scared, I told myself. Scared of Stephanie. Scared of losing his daughter. She'd been testing her wings, but he saw it as flight. Loss of her, of his control over her.

A car pulled into the driveway, then another, maybe more.

Lucas loosened his hold at the sound, then chomped Huntoon's arm.

I wondered if I could squeeze the trigger if I had to; my arm felt dead from keeping the gun on Huntoon.

Steffie looked over my shoulder.

"It's the police," she said.

They flooded in behind me, guns drawn.

They handcuffed Huntoon, read him his rights from a little card.

Stephanie sat on the floor, her face in her hands, unable to look or talk.

Huntoon was being conciliatory again. "It's a mistake," he said. "She broke into the house. I was afraid she was going to hurt my daughter. A man's got a right to protect his daughter, doesn't he? He's king of the castle, isn't he?"

I gave a cop my gun. Huntoon's, that is.

They took my statement while I sat on the front hall steps, Lucas's head in my lap. Stephanie sat on the peach-colored sofa in the living room for hers, underneath her sweet sixteen portrait. She held her body the same way she had for the painting: legs crossed at the ankles and held to one side, hands folded in her lap, her head slightly tilted.

The cop who was writing her statement reached over once and touched her hand. I wondered if he had kids.

When I'd finished talking I stood and stared at her through the French doors, her crest of hair bobbing up and down against the painting's gold leaf frame. Her jeans were worn through at the knees. Her sweater, a pale green cardigan, was dingy at the elbows and frayed at the cuffs.

So this is who Jack saw in the bus window, I told myself, before she got this hairdo. Maybe he's not such a nut case after all.

Stephanie saw me looking at the sweater and pulled it closer around her body. I wondered if it was the same one Andrea had owned and how Stephanie had gotten it. I decided it wasn't right to ask.

After a while the cops who were talking to her left the room.

I stepped in.

"Go ahead," she said to me.

"Go ahead what?"

"Take my picture. I can see from your eyes it's what you want to do. Besides, I want to see your camera. It's stuffed in your jacket, isn't it?"

I unzipped the zipper halfway and pulled out my Leica.

Stephanie sat absolutely still on the sofa and looked directly into the lens. I shot one from where I stood, then backed up and shot another.

She smiled. "That's what I use, too," she said. "A Leica. He"—she glanced toward the front hall, as though Huntoon were still there—"he wanted to get me a Hasselblad or something, but I bought a Leica. Myself."

"Were those your pictures? The ones of the stripper?"

She flushed. Ears, cheeks, even the shaved part of her head.

Of course they were.

"I found them in the condo," I told her. "They're pretty good, Stephanie. Andrea must have been glad you gave them to her. What did she say?"

The girl went silent. Her eyes filled with tears, but she willed them away.

Seventeen, I thought. Maybe eighteen. A bad age. She pulled her legs underneath her.

Ready to fly the coop but not sure where to land.

Her hands looked like a little kid's: bitten fingernails, ink stains.

"I don't know," she said. "She never said anything about them."

I pulled my wallet out of my jacket and handed her the poem I'd found, still folded small.

"And you wrote this to her too, didn't you? You wanted her to know about you; you wanted to know what you had in common, was that it?"

She touched the paper to her cheek.

"You know," I said, "I thought it was something Andrea had written. Your handwriting's just the same. It's odd, isn't it? My brother's handwriting looked just like my dad's." I wondered if mine looked anything like my mother's. I wished I had something she'd written.

Lucas came into the room, his toenails clicking on the marble floor. He sniffed Stephanie, making sure she was okay, then lay down with his head on my feet.

She sighed. "I only ever talked to her on the phone. I wanted to meet her someplace sometime, but she said—"

"She wasn't ready."

"That's right."

The phone conversation Pamela Minnick overheard.

"At first," she said, "I don't think she believed me. She said she never had a daughter. Then she told me they told her the baby had died. She had me when she was seventeen. In a place some nuns ran in New Hampshire. She hung up on me the first time I called. And then—"

"What?"

"I was worried about my mother. My adoptive mother. She's been good to me all my life. I didn't want to hurt her. I was afraid to tell her at first because I didn't want to hurt her."

"You must have been confused."

"Yeah," she said. "Confused. And then my"—she choked on the word—"my dad—*he* started following me around. I wasn't doing very well in school. I wasn't working on my college applications. He thought I was doing drugs. He bought a home lie detector test from a magazine—"

I got a baffling craving for Max. He was unreliable but he wasn't mean, he never in my life—

"And he thinks you can buy anything," she said. "At first he told me he'd buy me a bunch of equipment—lights, telephoto lenses, all kinds of junk—if I wouldn't talk to Andrea. He tried to pay one of my boyfriends off once, too, to keep him away from me. I thought he was going to try to pay Andrea to say she wasn't my mother. But what he did was he paid the guard at the courthouse—"

She covered her eyes with her hands. "I saw him," she said. "I saw him take the money out of his safe and give it to the guard the night before he killed her. Andrea never told anybody at the courthouse she was sick. The guard and my dad made that all up, and they dragged them out of the courthouse, too. That guy LeClair was in handcuffs. It wouldn't have been hard. I didn't know what to do. So I—"

"You what?"

"So I ran away."

"To where?"

"Some friends. And then he really started following me around. He's good at it. He borrows cars from people. He saw me leave a note on Andrea's car; I figured that out. I was afraid—"

"Of what?"

"That I was pushing her too hard. I wanted to talk to her real bad. I didn't want to move in with her or anything. My adoptive mother is my mother. But Andrea was worried, she said. She was like—"

She choked up again, then caught herself.

"She was kind of like my dad that way. Afraid it would hurt my mother. She said she was glad I'd had a good mother. She said she was glad I'd had a decent life."

"Was it?"

"What?"

"Was it a decent life?"

She looked around the room, then raised her hand as though she were going to tuck her hair behind her ear. Except there wasn't any hair.

She dropped her hand to her lap.

"Yeah," she said. "It's been okay. My mother has been good to me. She pushes for me to do things. She gets happy for me when I make something or figure something out. My dad— he's made cracks all my life about how hard it was going to be to find someone to marry me."

Max used to say the same about me.

"But my mom," she said, "she wants me to be somebody. She made me work in school; talked me out of trying to be a cheerleader. She likes to look at my pictures. She likes to talk about them, even."

She stood up. The setting sun came through the picture window at the front of the room, glazing the furniture and the floors an apricot color, throwing Stephanie's shadow across the rug.

It occurred to me that she might not know that Andrea had been a photographer, too.

"Hey," I said, "Did you know that—"

"Sorry," she said. "The cops are going to the Y to get Mom. I've got to go with them. She'll need me there."

"Of course she will."

215

26

In the aftermath of her father's arrest, Stephanie and I promised to write to each other, promised to be friends, promised to stay in touch. She came to the last seminar I gave, this time with a shorter, sleeker Mohawk, sat at the back of the room, and listened hard. We had sandwiches in my office afterward.

"You could have joined in, you know," I told her. "You shouldn't have let the others intimidate you. I'll bet you have plenty of interesting things to say."

She brushed off the comment with a wave of her hand, then reached into her backpack and pulled out an orange Agfa-Gevaert box, like the ones every photographer I know stores prints in.

"Here," she said. "I brought you these."

She lifted out a stack of prints and set them on my desk.

"I do this better than I talk."

They were pictures of downtown Boston. One was of an empty curbside parking space, a makeshift METER DOESN'T WORK sign taped to the meter head.

"That's where I first saw Andrea," she said. "That's where she parked her car that day."

Another was of an empty table in a coffee shop, dust motes floating in the column of light just above it.

"And that one—" she said, "is of the coffee shop I followed her to. I'd almost gotten up the nerve to talk to her, but I chickened out. So I watched her from the window. She had a bran muffin with butter on it, and she gave the guy at the next table her newspaper when she left."

She blew a fleck of something off the print.

"It's funny," she said. "It's the things like that I remember. A pat of butter. The newspaper."

There was a picture of the front stoop on Fayerweather Street, and another of a set of elevator doors in the downstairs lobby of the building Darling and Ueland is in. They were almost, but not quite, closed.

"That's the last time I saw her," she said. "It was her back. She'd just stepped in."

The pictures were somber, unsparing of the city's grime and litter. But they had a tenderness to them—an elegiac softness.

The last was of the top floors of the office building in an early evening drizzle, taken at an angle that made it look nearly majestic, like an ocean liner prow in the fog, the lights in the windows shining like strands of jewels.

"How in the world did you get that?" I asked her. "Were you hanging from a helicopter?"

"No," she said. "I talked a maintenance man at a building on Washington Street into letting me up on his roof."

"You ought to be careful about stuff like that, Stephanie," I chided her. "You ought—"

What was I talking about? I was the one who had walked backward into traffic on Mass. Ave. that very morning to get a picture of an oncoming motorcycle.

"Forget it," I said.

She zipped up her jacket, patted Lucas on the head, and turned to leave.

"Don't forget these, Stephanie." I held the box toward her. "They're—" I couldn't think of the right adjective. Beautiful? Strong? Evocative? They were all clichés, and they were all wrong.

"They're good work, Stephanie," I told her.

She shrugged, then smiled a little.

"They're for you," she said, and left.

I haven't heard from her since. No, I take that back. She left two messages on my machine one afternoon a couple of months after I moved back to New York. In the first one she told me that she and a friend wanted to come to Manhattan for the weekend and stay with me. In the second she told me that they'd changed their minds—that they'd decided to go to Florida instead. Or, she added, maybe Mexico.

I got a huge kick out of those messages and didn't erase them for a long time. New York? No, Miami. Or Mexico maybe. I played them for Claire when she came to visit with baby Arthur, burbling in his baby container.

"Remember those days, Claire?" I asked her. "Remember when you were a kid and the world seemed that small, that easy to tame? New York, she says. No, Miami. Mexico, maybe. I love it."

But Claire was barely conscious of me. She didn't respond, didn't even look up. She probably hadn't even heard the tape. She was that utterly, irretrievably lost in her bald-headed boy.

BM